Advance Praise for

MURDER
beyond the
PRECIPICE

Haunted by frightening dreams, Elizabeth Pennington returns to her past and journeys to a spooky, not-what-it-seems Maine resort. Her anticipated pleasant weekend takes a deadly turn when she is menaced by dire warnings, a missing friend, and more.

Things get worse when she becomes the target of an obsessive killer.

Filled with colorful characters who make an interesting mix, the mood of the tale can suddenly go from sunny and breezy to dark and terrifying. *Murder beyond the Precipice* is a fun, captivating mystery.

—Dale T. Phillips, Author of the Zack Taylor Mysteries

MURDER
beyond the
PRECIPICE

PENNY GOETJEN

SECRET
HARBOR
PRESS

For information about this title or to order other books and/or electronic media, contact the publisher:
Secret Harbor Press, LLC
www.secretharborpress.com

Library of Congress Control Number: 2018905110

Printed in the United States of America

Publisher's Cataloging-In-Publication Data
(Prepared by The Donohue Group, Inc.)

Names: Goetjen, Penny.

Title: Murder beyond the precipice / Penny Goetjen.

Description: [Charleston, South Carolina] : Secret Harbor Press, [2018]

Identifiers: ISBN 9780997623567 (print) | ISBN 9780997623574 (ebook) | ISBN 9780997623581 (audiobook)

Subjects: LCSH: Women interior decorators--Maine--Boothbay Harbor--Fiction. | Missing persons--Maine--Boothbay Harbor--Fiction. | Murder--Investigation--Maine--Boothbay Harbor--Fiction. | Bed and breakfast accommodations--Maine--Boothbay Harbor--Fiction. | Families--Maine--Boothbay Harbor--Fiction. | LCGFT: Detective and mystery fiction.

Classification: LCC PS3607.O3355 M872 2018 (print) | LCC PS3607.O3355 (ebook) | DDC 813/.6--dc23

To all the loyal readers who demanded
a sequel to Murder on the Precipice
so you could accompany Elizabeth
on another escapade.

CHAPTER ONE

*C*lenched *fists dangled* at his sides. He stared blankly at the atrocity sprawled in front of him, lying still as if in restful sleep. If only it were true. He couldn't undo the work of his strong hands, still aching from holding on so tight. Now he would have to take care of the mess.

Stretching out his fingers, he examined them closely, turning his palms over and then face down again. Bulging red knuckles. Veins that protruded on top. Creases that cut curiously across the palms. There were no calluses. No discernible scars other than the raised jagged line that curved around the base of his thumb where he'd undergone stitches as a youngster after a fight, but no evidence the hands could have performed such a grisly act.

Shoving a hand deep into his pocket, a wad of keys jingled as he pulled them out. Slipping the metal ring onto his first two fingers, his gaze wandered out the windows as he twirled the ring effortlessly around. Once. Twice. Three times and then back into his pocket again. Like a cowboy spinning his revolver after a shoot-out and re-holstering it.

Padding across the worn Oriental rug, he adjusted the temperature on the thermostat as low as it would go, then slipped through the old wooden door, locking it securely behind him. No one could be allowed in. Not until he made things right again. For now, there was blood on the stairs that needed to be tended to.

The musty air caught in his nose, creating a wrinkle on the bridge. Surveying the space lit only by a single bulb hanging from the ceiling where the sides of the roof met at the highest point, he weighed his options in the narrow swath of his flashlight. An old buggy once used for horse-drawn carriage rides on cool summer evenings filled one dark corner. Next to it was an antique sleigh whose useful life ended with a broken runner many years earlier. It would have been ideal to dig the hole under one of those half-forgotten vehicles, but he would need help moving them away from the corner and back again. Eager to get started, he decided on an area next to the far wall where tools hung neatly.

The dirt was hard packed, cool, and gritty, and the digging arduous. Not what he was used to doing. He hoped it would only take a couple nights, only daring to dig when the rest of the town was asleep. Padlocked doors during the day. No one in. No stupid questions to answer.

Shovelful after shovelful, he thrust the blade into the soil, scooping and heaving it onto the pile. The hole began to take shape. The depth was more important than the other dimensions. Shovel in, dirt out. The mound grew taller. Throughout the night he toiled, leaving the door open a crack so he would see the first sign of morning light. A couple feet in, he ran into rocks; some mere pebbles, others the size of his fist. They trickled down from the top of the pile after he tossed them.

Fluttering above his head drew his eyes away from his task. A barn owl had returned from a night of prowling, slipping in through the missing slats in the vent at the top of the eaves. Inspecting his work, he decided he'd dug more than halfway. Done until the next night.

Wiping sweat from his brow, he shoved a hand deep into his pocket and pulled out a ring of keys. Slipping it onto his left hand, he sized up the pile of rocks and dirt as he twirled it around his first two fingers. Once. Twice. Three times and then back in again.

The click of the lock releasing within the door made him jump, terrified someone had heard. Pushing open the old panel, wood scraping on wood, his body stiffened as it creaked on its hinges. Stepping inside, he pushed it closed behind him and crossed the room, fumbling for the switch on the bedside lamp. Flinching at the sudden brightness, his eyes shot straight to the pillows. The most gruesome part of the task lay ahead. But it would all be over soon.

Inching nearer, he dared a closer look. Time did strange things to a dead body. Probably better that way. He could pretend it was someone else. Someone he didn't know. There was less of a connection that way. A shiver ripped through his body from the chill in the air, ripe with a sour odor. Fortunately there was no blood to clean up. His rash move hadn't involved a knife or any other sharp object. He had relied on his strong hands fueled by the fury that burst inside him. Cleanup would be relatively straightforward. He pulled the bottom sheet up and wrapped it around the body, reserving the top one for later.

The laundry cart had proved useful. Probably had never carried that much weight before but was handling it fairly well. The steering on it could use work, but then again it wasn't designed for carrying human remains. Guiding it down the slate walkway, in spite of his best efforts, he struggled to keep the cart on the stepping-stones. It veered off onto the grass halfway to the carriage house. Swearing he'd drag it if the wheels fell off, he yanked it back on track and up to the double doors, bolted securely on the outside. Guiding the key into the padlock, he turned it, listening for the soft click. Sliding a panel to the side, he pushed the cart up to the crude hole he'd dug. Not very deep, but deep enough. Not perfectly rectangular, but close enough.

CHAPTER ONE

Laying a sheet down on the ground so the outside of the cart wouldn't get soiled when he tipped it, he put his weight behind the far end only to realize he couldn't lift it up toward the hole like the bed of a dump truck. It just rolled on its wheels. Hitting a snag so close to finishing the grim task was regrettable. Rethinking his approach, he positioned himself between the hole and the cart, wedging one foot up next to a front wheel. Certain he could tilt the cart with the newfound leverage, he grabbed the top lip and pulled. His fingers slipped off, and the momentum propelled him backward. Landing with a soft thud, he groaned as his body hit the hard dirt. Dull pain roared with a white flash through his head.

Furious to be lying flat on his back in the hole meant for the deceased, he clambered his way up the side, digging the toes of his shoes in the dirt wall to get a foothold as he climbed. Once he'd swung his legs over the top and stood up again, he assessed the amount of dirt covering his front side, figuring the back looked as bad. Not to be outdone by a hole he'd dug or the damn laundry cart, he lunged for the back rim. Grabbing on tightly and fueled by anger, he shoved it. Feet slipping under him, he turned sideways and propped his crouching body up against the side and pushed. Gradually it moved as he used his feet to brace.

Once the front wheels cleared the edge, he gave the cart one last shove and then turned to watch it tumble to the bottom, landing upside down, concealing its contents. Grateful he didn't have to look at it any longer, he snatched the handle of the shovel sticking out of the pile, threw in the sheet that had served no purpose, and started refilling the hole.

Settling into a rhythm scooping the dirt back in, he damned the two that had caused him the manual labor. At first the dirt made a hollow thud but soon softened as the cart disappeared from sight. Shovelful after shovelful, the hole slowly filled. Wiping his forehead, he did his best to tamp down the loose soil to try to make it look undisturbed but quickly discovered that was next to impossible. And despite his efforts, he had extra dirt left over he didn't know what to do with.

Spying a wheelbarrow next to the hanging tools, he loaded it up and pushed it to the far corner of the gardens and dumped it, making four trips. Returning the shovel to the proper place, he shoved a hand deep into his pocket and fingered his keys.

The dirty deed was finally complete. Relief and exhaustion coursed through him. Not particularly fond of physical labor, his back ached and his throat was parched. Time for a celebratory drink.

Quickly washing up and changing out of his dirt-caked clothes, he slipped back to the room to straighten it with clean sheets taken from housekeeping's closet. Noticing he'd forgotten to remove the pillowcases when he pulled the sheets, he peeled them off without much thought and tossed them into the trash can outside the small bathroom.

After opening the French doors, he pulled out his keys. Slipping them onto the first two fingers of his left hand, his gaze wandered to the gardens as he twirled the ring around. Once. Twice. Three times and then back in his pocket again.

Securing the door behind him, he then returned the key to the slot at the front desk.

CHAPTER TWO

Elizabeth *could hear* ringing from the foot of the stairs and bolted to the landing in a few quick strides. Plunging her hand into the satchel-style purse hanging by a strap on her shoulder, she rummaged frantically to retrieve the key. Desperate to grab the phone before the answering machine picked up, she turned her bag upside down and dumped the contents onto the floor; a hard cased wallet, her cell phone with a black and white damask cover, a black and white toile compact umbrella, a small package of tissues, wadded-up loose tissues, a small black leather make-up bag, individually wrapped peppermint candies, and a colorful silk scarf abandoned on an unusually hot day and left to get wrinkled in the bottom of her bag. As she scanned the pile, it crossed her mind that commercial-grade carpet in a public hallway was undoubtedly quite filthy, but it dissipated into a fleeting thought. Poking up through the middle of the heap was the end of a pink and white polka-dotted ribbon. She knelt down and grabbed it, jerking it free. A corner of her mouth turned upward at the single key dangling from the other end. With it securely grasped in her fingers, she lunged toward the knob.

How many times had it rung already? Having opened her design studio nine months earlier, she couldn't afford a receptionist yet and was trying to manage without any other support staff. There were times, though, she wished she could step out to run an errand, grab lunch, or meet a client without worrying her office phone was unattended. Elizabeth knew how important it was for calls to be handled promptly and with the personal touch of a live person. Someday it would happen. . . .

In her haste, the key kept striking all around the narrow slit in the knob, and when it did hit its mark, it only penetrated slightly and then was met with resistance. She had unlocked the door dozens of times, perhaps hundreds, yet suddenly she couldn't get the key to work. Willing the phone to keep ringing, she tried flipping the key over, and then it eased into place. Shoving open the door, she dashed across the small lobby to the receptionist's desk, catching a toe on the area rug but recovering nicely. She snatched the receiver from the cradle.

"Pennington Design Associates," Elizabeth spoke firmly but gently and with a lilt in her voice. She pressed the black plastic handle to her ear. Silence. Click. Dial tone.

Returning the receiver, Elizabeth closed her eyes and grabbed onto the front edge of the desk, bracing her slender body against it. She drew in a lungful of stale office air, which she held for a few seconds and then released. There'd been a few too many calls lately where the person at the other end hung up when she answered, making her feel quite unsettled.

Snippets of a recurring dream flashed through her head. In it, a white unmarked commercial van appeared regularly from behind her. At the sound of screeching tires, she would turn to see the van barreling straight for her. She'd wake up before it made contact, in a cold sweat and gasping for breath. As with most dreams, it didn't make sense, but the sheer number of times it occurred and the obvious intention of the driver terrified her. *What did it mean?*

Elizabeth pushed away thoughts that the hang-ups and dreams could be related to the prior summer. One thing was certain; she'd been working too hard, and it was time for a change of scenery. But it was going to take more than a walk around the block.

Slipping a cream-colored envelope out from under the gooseneck lamp, she smirked as she flipped open the flap and slipped out the contents. It was her ticket out of town. An unexpected invitation to a high school friend's wedding on the coast of Maine. It had traveled quite a distance with multiple forwarding labels before it found Elizabeth's new location in Connecticut. As she examined it more closely, she realized the wedding and reception were to be held at the same inn where her friend Rashelle now worked. The appointed time of the wedding was a scant twenty-four hours away. Reluctant to take time out of her busy schedule and make the trip for someone she was never close to, Elizabeth had procrastinated returning the RSVP card. Obviously too late to gain entrance to the reception, she could at least go to the ceremony. Surely Shelle would let her stay at her place. She'd been pressing her for a while to make the trip to visit her at her new job. Lizzi, as her friends called her, hadn't taken any vacation days since she hung out her shingle the previous fall, and perhaps it was a good time to do it.

Elizabeth decided she would surprise her friend with an unexpected visit. It was a beautiful Friday afternoon in early June, and a weekend away from the stresses of launching a new business would be revitalizing. And although it was uncharacteristically spur-of-the-moment, she was going home.

Letting out a cathartic breath, Elizabeth allowed her shoulders to droop. When her head followed, her shoulder-length, silky brown hair jostled slightly. She held this position until she suddenly felt as if she was being watched. Pivoting toward the door, she looked into a set of deep, dark eyes staring intently at her.

The sweet face belonged to a black Lab mix with a sleek shiny coat sitting obediently with his royal blue leash dangling to one side. He was waiting for her to give the signal to come in. She'd nearly forgotten he'd been by her side as she scampered up the stairs to her second-floor studio. He'd been her constant companion since she rescued him from the local animal shelter a few months earlier. She would never forget that day.

She'd always longed for the companionship of a loyal dog, but living in New York City and working such long hours for her previous boss weren't conducive to owning a pup. Now that she was making the rules, she'd decided it was time to let a warm, loving, four-legged spirit into her life.

Elizabeth had entered the shelter filled with excitement, anxiety, and hope all swirling around inside. Walking up and down the rows of metal cages, her excitement turned to a pit in her stomach, though. The sheer number of dogs that needed rescuing was overwhelming. She wished she could rescue every single one of them and grappled with the realization she couldn't. The dog in each cage looked up at her, as if imploring her to take him/her home. Some got up when she approached, wagging their tails to great her. Others just looked up from where they lay, as if they'd already given up on being adopted. Rescuing a dog was much more difficult than she'd expected. She wished she could take them all home. At the end of a long row of cages, she stopped.

Standing alert at the front of his cage was a handsome black dog that looked like a young pup with room to grow into his oversized paws. He sat down, maintaining his gaze, looking deep inside of her as if he was evaluating her soul. She felt drawn to him. He put a humorously large paw against the chain-link gate of his container, and she pressed her hand against the warm pads on the underside of it. In spite of the metal grating between them, they made a connection.

She couldn't wait for the approval process to be over so she could bring the sweet dog home. After a few days, "Buddy" was officially rescued and happily became Elizabeth's forever friend. He adapted very quickly to her two-bedroom condo that was within walking distance of her office.

After picking up a few things for herself and Buddy for the weekend, Elizabeth was finally heading back to Maine. She hadn't been there since the end of last summer when a Category 4

hurricane wreaked havoc on Pennington Point Inn, her childhood home. It had been a struggle for her to leave behind the carnage, and she'd been unable to drag herself back—not only because of her workload but also because the pain was still too raw. Since then, she'd walked away from her design career in Manhattan and started anew in Connecticut. It was a scary step, yet one she'd dreamed of taking since college. All the years she'd worked for her former boss Vera Loran at Loran Design, she desperately wanted to set out on her own. After a relatively brief search, she found quaint West Hartford had a downtown that fit her desire to be able to live and work within walking distance. To her, it was like a miniature Manhattan, so that made the transition a little easier. She parked her car in the garage under the building her condo was in and rarely took it out, walking to just about everything she needed; restaurants, bars, her favorite grocery store, a movie theater, and clothing boutiques. She was centrally located with New York City to the west and Boston to the east, a couple of hours by car either way.

During the previous several months, Elizabeth had worked very hard to build a clientele. She'd had no idea what to expect after cutting ties with her former job and was pleased the launch of her design business turned out much better than she'd expected, though far from profitable yet. Thankfully Elizabeth's design talent, reputation, references, and experience carried her. The cold calls were the toughest part, but she was willing to do whatever was necessary to make her business successful. Now, after logging in very long hours for several months, she was looking forward to a well-earned break and catching up with her friend.

Rashelle had been the assistant manager of Pennington Point Inn before the destructive storm abruptly rendered her, and everyone else who worked there, unemployed. While she spent several months searching for something steady, she went from one bartending job to another until finally landing a manager position at an inn in the Boothbay region. Renovations were underway with the expectation it would open soon to the public. Apparently they were able to do a soft opening to accommodate the wedding. Elizabeth had laughed when Rashelle asked her if she knew where the inn was located. After all, Elizabeth grew up in Maine, albeit south of Boothbay, but she knew Maine quite well. Shelle was the outsider, a transplant from Brooklyn.

Buddy was curled up on the passenger seat of her prized BMW Z4, the sporty little car that was Elizabeth's pride and joy, a reward she'd given herself during the years of working long hours at Loran Design. She loved driving it, particularly since it was a six-speed manual transmission. Unfortunately, in true sports car fashion, it only had two seats, and Buddy was clearly taking up every inch of his. Elizabeth acknowledged that once he was full grown, she would have to consider trading in her impractical car for something with a little more room so her canine friend could be comfortable sprawled across the back seat. She couldn't imagine going anywhere without him.

CHAPTER THREE

The inn was quiet, too quiet for Rashelle's liking. It felt like she was alone in the sprawling structure, but she hoped it was just because she was the only one in the west wing. It was an old building steeped in history, one she was reluctantly starting to learn more about. Fellow employees were only too eager to fill her in on what allegedly transpired under its roof, particularly during the years before it became an inn. Talk of unusual late-night happenings was a bit unsettling to her. The stories included beer taps suddenly turning on behind the bar, lights turning on after they'd been turned off for the night, and the clunk, clunk of boots walking on hardwood in the second-floor corridor, even though it had been carpeted years earlier. She hadn't yet decided if she believed all the tales.

A few last-minute checks around the inn and then Rashelle would be able to leave it all behind and head out for the weekend. Couldn't happen soon enough. She'd been working her ass off but in a capacity more along the lines of a construction site foreman. Not what she'd signed on for. If she hadn't been so desperate for a job, she would have told the owner to f**k off and left long ago. The fact of the matter was Rashelle *was* desperate. When she finally got the job offer, her credit cards were maxed out, and her landlord was in the process of evicting her from her cramped, grimy loft. She was one step away from living out of her car. Her mother, if she were still alive, would have been mortified. How had it gotten so bad? She stopped short of blaming it on the alcohol. It was her escape and gave her something to look forward to in her sad, shortsighted life.

As she made a final pass through the kitchen, scanning to make sure nothing was out of place, she noticed a case of wine delivered that day but still sitting next to the back door. She was tempted to snag a bottle and walk out with it in her purse—payback for the bullshit she'd put up with—but decided the repercussions for getting caught were not worth a lousy bottle of wine, even if it was a vintage well beyond her means. Hell, they were all beyond her means, but she wasn't going to let that stop her from having fun. It was Friday night, and she had plans to catch up with newfound friends at her regular hangout. Her loins throbbed at the thought of the hot guy she'd met there last weekend. His dark, wavy hair caught her eye, and she'd walked right up and engaged him. She could still feel his strong arm around her waist as they swayed to slow songs. God, she hoped he was there again tonight. If he was, she was leaving there with him, no matter what she had to do to make it happen.

Her boss was adamant about keeping wine stored at a precise temperature. So she turned back, dropped her cell phone and keys on the counter and bent down to pick up the case of merlot with a grunt. Just as quickly, she released it. Clearly she couldn't carry the whole case at once. And there would be hell to pay if she broke any. She removed six bottles and placed them on the floor. Bending her knees, she easily picked up the box and headed toward the wine cellar at the back of the kitchen. Balancing it on one hip, she maneuvered the tricky latch. Finally she got the door unlocked and pulled it open wide enough so she had time to turn in and let it hit her on her backside. Flipping the light switch just inside, she headed down the stairs, letting the door bang shut behind her.

A few feet from the bottom of the stairs were several unfinished wooden racks lined up along the wall with rows upon rows of wine, all organized in alphabetical order by vineyard within the type of wine. She plucked each bottle from the box and added it to the racks in the appropriate slots. When the box was empty, she headed back upstairs and reloaded it with the other half. She went through the same routine to re-enter the wine cellar with the remaining bottles. This time the door shut like before but with the unmistakable click of the latch behind her as she descended the stairs.

After inserting the remaining six bottles, she headed back up with the empty box in one hand and flipped the light switch with the other, immersing her into complete darkness as her hand pressed against the door. It hit a hard, immovable surface. Frowning, she transferred the box to her other side and flipped the light switch back on. She raised the latch and pushed hard again. It wouldn't give. Trying desperately not to panic, Rashelle lifted the latch as high as she could and lunged at it with her shoulder. It wouldn't budge. She tried pulling the handle toward her and lifting the latch to see if it would go any higher before pushing but was unable to make it move any more than it had before. She pounded on the door, knowing there was a good chance there was no one around to hear her. Or had someone deliberately shut her in the cellar? Were those footsteps crossing the kitchen floor?

"Hey! Come back here. Let me out. This isn't funny. Let me out," she bellowed, her voice cracking.

Before long, the side of her fist began to ache, so she held up for a moment. She reached for the back pocket on her jeans only to realize her phone was sitting on the counter. Slowly she turned around and plopped down on the top step, contemplating what to do to get herself out of the tight spot. She threw the empty cardboard box down the steps in disgust, watching as it tumbled down the rudimentary wooden treads, bouncing a couple times on the dirt floor before coming to rest against the racks. The stones that made up the old cellar wall caught her eye. She'd never noticed them before and decided they were quite beautiful. They reminded her of the stones in the wine cellar at Pennington Point Inn.

CHAPTER FOUR

N*early giddy about hitting* the road for a weekend away, Elizabeth maneuvered her Z4 through the streets of West Hartford, grinning as she imagined Rashelle's reaction when she showed up unannounced at the inn's doorstep. Making one stop at her favorite bagel place, she picked up an "everything" bagel with vegetable cream cheese and a couple plain bagel sticks for Buddy.

Merging onto Interstate 84 was like trying to join a swiftly moving school of fish. It took just the right timing to slip between two cars whose drivers had no intention of making room for anyone else. As she neared Hartford, traffic slowed down. It was approaching rush hour on a Friday afternoon, so they crawled through the intersection with I-91.

By the time the Z4 emerged on the other side of Hartford, Elizabeth's hopes of picking up speed were dashed by the volume of cars leaving the city and heading east. It was times like this she didn't particularly enjoy having a manual shift car. There was a lot of downshifting as traffic slowed, shifting back up when the speed picked up again, and over again. She endured several more minutes of slow-moving traffic before it finally opened up, and she shifted into sixth. At the crinkling of the white paper bag, Buddy lifted his head and thumped his tail against the back of the seat. The two happily nibbled on their yummy snack, passing the time as they munched.

A half an hour on I-84 brought them to the Massachusetts Turnpike, which she merged onto heading east. At the first rest stop at Charlton, she pulled off and slipped into a parking spot on the far end of the lot. There were no other cars near her since, per usual, the dog run was located in a remote area. As Buddy took care of business, she scanned the area, grateful it was still light out. Sensing movement in her peripheral vision, she caught a blur of white heading down an aisle, popping in and out of view between a line of parked cars as it passed. With tingly fingers she grabbed her pup's leash to prepare to run for the car. As she maintained her line of sight on the vehicle, she realized it was a pickup truck, not a commercial van as she'd feared.

Cursing her dreams, she moved the car closer to the entrance, leaving the windows down a few inches on each side. She dashed inside to grab a coffee from the donut shop and a package of something sweet from the vending machine, staples for a long-distance car ride.

Back on the road again, Elizabeth ripped into the Twizzlers package and pulled out a couple slim red twists. Buddy raised his head and sniffed in her direction, so she tore off another piece of bagel stick for him.

"You're a good boy, Buddy." As he chewed voraciously, she patted the top of his head. She was tickled to have him with her. She never knew what she was missing before he'd arrived.

As the sun dropped in her rearview mirror, Elizabeth progressed farther east. Just as it touched the horizon, she took the exit for Interstate 495. Changing to a new highway always made her feel as though she was making significant progress. She reached over to surf the radio, landing on an oldies station playing a familiar Bee Gees tune.

Her energy level began to wane, so she reached for the Styrofoam cup wedged into the drink holder between the two seats and drained the last couple drops from it, regretting her choice of a small instead of a large. She pressed on. Finally she spotted the first sign for Interstate 95, which perked her up.

"We're getting close to Maine, Buddy. We're getting there!" He cocked his head with a look of curiosity on his sweet face.

At the end of I-495, Elizabeth connected onto I-95 north, crossing the Massachusetts line into New Hampshire before too long. Passing the Portsmouth rotary that led to the outlets, the familiar Piscataqua River Bridge came into view in the distance. With three lanes on each side and its green metal span, the iconic bridge connected Portsmouth to Kittery, Maine. Driving across the suspended roadway, tingling returned to her fingers. Sneaking a glance off to the right, she could see the sad, rusty remains of the old bridge standing awkwardly in the river, unattached and deserted. A lasting reminder of days gone by. Halfway across the bridge, a sign declared she had officially crossed the border where the highway transitioned from being the New Hampshire Turnpike to the Maine Turnpike.

There was something special about being in Maine. The air was somehow lighter, cleaner, perhaps more inspiring. The frenetic pace of life endured by those in the lower New England states was left behind and replaced with a much slower, more deliberate way of carrying on. She felt a certain air of expectation that bordered on animated excitement. For Elizabeth, it had been too long since she'd been back to Maine. Far too long.

As soon as her tires reached dry land on the other side, she let out a squeal and shared her excitement with her furry friend. "We're in Maine, Buddy!"

He sat up and joined in the excitement, letting out a solitary bark.

Elizabeth laughed and stroked the soft, warm fur on his back. He remained upright and looked out the windows as if surveying the scenery passing swiftly by, trying to determine what Maine was all about. He sniffed the air, perhaps detecting the unfamiliar brine.

"Can you smell the ocean, big guy? We'll definitely have to check out one of my favorite beaches while we're here. You're going to have so much fun running on the soft sand and figuring out the waves. I have to warn you, though. The water is really cold. You won't want to be in it long," she cautioned. "Ooooh, I bet you'd love the taste of lobster, too. You can't visit Maine for the first time without trying lobster. It's too early for wild blueberries, which is too bad. Oh and raspberries, too. Both are amazing, but they don't come out until about mid-summer."

He gazed affectionately in her direction, thumping his tail against the door, listening to every word.

Not far across the border, Elizabeth pulled off into the visitors' center to take a short break, splitting her trip into thirds. After a quick visit to the dog run, she pulled out Buddy's dish and fed him his dinner. He didn't seem to care he was eating to the roar of traffic whizzing by. On their way back to the car she grabbed a bottled ice tea, passing on the idea of getting something hot from a vending machine, shuddering at the thought of what that would have tasted like. How often were those machines cleaned and refilled? Once settled back in the car, she pulled out of the slot and noticed a white commercial van pulling up in her rearview mirror. She kept an eye on it until it pulled in a few cars away. There was nothing painted on the side. Were her dreams making her paranoid? She stepped on the gas and sped down the entrance ramp, leaving the troubling thought behind. Back on the highway, the waning evening light gave way to darkness.

Elizabeth stayed on I-95 as it curved north and then northnortheast, roughly following along the southern coast of Maine. Green highway signs pointed out exits for York, Ogunquit, Kennebunkport, Old Orchard Beach, and Portland, eliciting visions from her childhood of clambakes on the beach, steamed local lobsters, and wild blueberries sold along local roads. Just north of Portland, the Pennington Point signs started to appear, looming above the highway. She sat back slightly in her seat.

Images of shuttered windows and broken fixtures from last summer's tragedy washed away her warm fuzzy memories. Her eyes welled, and she swallowed hard. She'd left it all behind with thoughts of rebuilding at some point but had no definitive plans in place. With her hands trembling on the wheel, the last sign reading "Pennington Point, Route 1, Access to Beaches" passed out of sight.

Oblivious to her heartache, her furry companion had settled back down, curled up on the passenger seat. He'd been spared the pain at her family's inn. She was grateful for that.

Several more miles passed under her tires before the first sign for the Boothbay Harbor Region appeared. Tired from a long week of work and hours on the road, Elizabeth was relieved they were getting close. Twenty miles or so on I-295 brought them onto a local road, passing strip malls and pausing for frequent traffic lights, on their way to Route 1.

Dramatically changing character along the way, Route 1 ran the length of the East Coast from Maine to the Florida Keys. They were picking it up near Brunswick in the form of a divided highway that lasted until just before Bath where it became a two-lane road. When they reached the bridge over the Kennebec River, Elizabeth glanced down and noticed the unmistakable shape of an imposing naval ship docked at Bath Iron Works. Route 1 continued to meander through small coastal towns, offering glimpses in the daylight of picturesque inlets along the way until it hooked up with Route 27 and headed down the hill to the quaint village of Wiscasset with its art galleries, antique stores, and B&Bs packed into a short span on the main street. The town was so small that if you hit the traffic light right and it wasn't the busy summer season with tourist traffic, you could easily go from one side to the other in less than three minutes.

On the other side of the bridge spanning the Back River, Route 1 continued on its merry way up the hill toward Rockland, but Elizabeth turned right to stay on 27. She fondly recalled a crouching tiger on the roof of a small gas station that used to be on the corner. Passing through Edgecomb, the two-lane road wound its way toward the coast for about ten miles and was dotted with modest homes, campsites, art galleries, a pottery studio, and miniature golf. The old train of Boothbay Railway Village was tucked away until the morning. As they got closer to town, she pressed the buttons to lower the windows and take in the salty sea air. It invigorated her body. She glanced over and noticed Buddy's nose flaring as he took in new smells.

"Pretty cool, huh Bud?"

Before long, they crested the hill atop Boothbay Harbor. Steeped in history with its origins firmly rooted in the fishing industry, the region enjoyed a brisk tourist business. It could get rather crowded during summer months, but with a little patience, it was tolerable. Being near the water made it all worthwhile. The sights and smells of the ocean were part of her soul after having grown up on the coast.

Instead of making a left to head directly to the inn, she decided to make a pass through downtown to have a look. The road split to the right in a one-way loop, and the first half was rather quiet, lined with private residences, the historical society, and a couple of inns. Approaching the heart of downtown, Elizabeth passed the post office on the left and the public library on the corner to the right. Reaching the stop sign, she was surprised to see the old bank building on the left currently housed a jewelry store but was relieved to see The Smiling Cow was still just down the hill in front of her.

The cheerful two-story, white clapboard house stood ready to greet visitors who ambled inside, unaware of the dizzying assortment of tourist-targeted treasures showcased within its walls. It was connected to Gimbel & Sons Country Store on the first floor so shoppers could wander between both establishments, browsing through vintage clothing, Maine-themed sweatshirts, pine-scented incense, one-of-a-kind gadgets, and memorable souvenirs, before exiting out the back onto the quaint wooden wharf.

Popular among tourists, the benches on the wharf were usually crowded with people resting their weary feet, eating a slice of pizza, or simply passing time until the rest of their family caught up. Others waited for the next boat to be called to take them on a seal watch or lighthouse tour.

Time stood still when Elizabeth and her grandmother, Amelia, sat on the wharf in the warm summer sun with an ice cream cone, one that was much too large for little Lizzi to finish and inevitably ended up getting tossed out. Little hands were wiped of the sticky aftermath before heading up the street to take in a game of candlepin bowling. Since the ball was much lighter and smaller than a traditional ball, and there were no huge holes to try to fit her tiny fingers in, she could grasp the ball with two hands, stand with her feet spread out wider than her shoulders, and roll it between her legs. Her grandmother shared in her excitement when she knocked down a pin or two. After bowling, they always made a stop just down the hill to buy fudge and salt water taffy. Sweet aromas wafted through the open door of the tiny shop. Only the strongest willed could walk past where the taffy pull machine was operating in one window and fudge was laid out in the other without stopping in to buy something.

Elizabeth suddenly realized she'd been idling a while and glanced into her rearview mirror, relieved to see no one behind her. She turned left, continuing down Townsend Avenue away from the town center, passing a handful of inns whose warm lighting indicated their guests had returned from their days' activities.

Just before reaching the end of Townsend, she turned right to pick up the road that ran along the edge of the harbor, stealing a glance between structures, happy to be so close to the water. Elizabeth remembered there were some beautiful homes along this stretch of the road that had great views, but she would have to wait until daylight to admire them. After about a mile, she approached Spruce Point and on the next curve saw the sign for The Inn on Boothbay Harbor, so she slowed as the entrance came into view. The first driveway was labeled "exit," but she pulled her car off to the side, directly across from it, so she could get a preview.

The inn was impressive in stature, a grand Victorian that seemed out-of-place in the quaint harbor town, sitting majestically on the property with strategically placed uplights spotlighting the façade. Sprawled in front of a dramatic two-story portico entrance were a circular driveway and an expansive lawn dotted with mature deciduous and evergreen trees. There were two rows of windows and a widow's walk three stories up that looked out onto unobstructed views of the harbor's calm waters, as if the inn had been keeping watch for generations. A carriage house was set to the left, accessed by an offshoot of the main drive. Two stone pillars framed the end of the driveway. "Livingston" was neatly etched on the front, a third of the way down. This was not exactly what she was picturing from the way Shelle had described it to her, but then again, the two friends rarely viewed life from the same perspective. Nevertheless, she thought the inn was absolutely beautiful.

Pulling ahead, she turned into the second driveway marked "entrance" and then straight into the parking lot off to the right. No need to pull up front; she would have to be somewhat furtive if she was going to surprise Rashelle. A few cars remained in the lot, and she hoped one of them was hers. Perhaps the rest belonged to staff, wedding guests, or various contractors working overtime to finish the renovations. Slipping hers into an end spot, she was relieved to have the long drive behind her and excited at the prospect of finding her friend.

Buddy sat up as she shut down the engine. Undoubtedly he'd had enough of the long ride and needed to stretch his canine legs. Elizabeth considered letting him go without a leash because he was so well behaved, and she felt he deserved it. But he was still a puppy and could be unpredictable at times, so she decided to err on the side of caution and clipped his leash onto his collar, vowing to make it up to him later.

With Buddy trotting along next to her, Elizabeth hastened up the stone walkway that curved toward the front entrance, gazing in awe at the building. Beautiful marble steps, worn in the center from years of use, led up to two carved wooden doors. A very grand entrance, indeed. It already had a very different feel from Pennington Point Inn. There was something about it that made Elizabeth feel rather uncomfortable, though. She did her best to shake off a feeling of foreboding, dismissing it as fatigue washing over her.

Stepping into a spacious two-story lobby that appeared to occupy the front half of the building, she resisted the temptation to see if her words could echo. An odd smell made her wrinkle her nose. Was it from recent renovations? Her pup's ears were alert, and his nose was taking it all in, too.

The space had a heavy, masculine feel to it. The navy blue print wallpaper and burgundy Oriental rug on the dark hardwood floor all but absorbed the limited light. The registration desk was set on the back wall to the right side. A graceful, curving mahogany stairway on the other side cascaded down from the second floor and splayed out at the bottom in dramatic fashion. A runner matching the rug ran up the middle of it. As they crossed, she admired a huge crystal chandelier she figured was original to the house. It sparkled even in the low light. Elizabeth took a quick look around to see if she could catch a glimpse of Rashelle.

A few people were gathered in conversation in the area to the right of the lobby. Elizabeth imagined they might refer to it as a drawing room or library in such a grand place. Others clanked dishes in a dining room to the left. Staff cleaning up after dinner or preparations for opening day?

Once at the reception desk, Buddy sat down obediently, and Elizabeth let go of his leash, resting one arm against the substantial counter. She could hear voices behind the door marked "office," so she hoped someone would eventually come out. They probably weren't expecting anyone. She casually wondered when the inn would be opening to the public. While she waited, she tried Rashelle's cell phone. It rang a few times and then went to voicemail. Elizabeth hung up without leaving a message, thinking she would rather catch her in person so she could really surprise her.

Finally the office door opened and a medium build, sandy-haired, twenty-something popped out from behind it. The sleeves of his white button-down shirt were rolled up to his elbows, like he'd just emerged from the trenches, and his distracted look said he wasn't sure what time of day it was. He stopped short when he noticed her. Elizabeth had hoped for a familiar face but trusted her expression didn't give away her disappointment.

"Good evening," she offered.

"Good evening. Checking in? . . . I'm sorry no one was at the front desk to greet you right away. I thought all the wedding guests had already checked in."

"Yes, I guess I've arrived later than is ideal. My apologies . . . wedding? Uh, yes, I am here for the wedding."

"I see."

"My good friend, Shelle, is your day manager. I'm Elizabeth Pennington. She actually doesn't know I'm coming. I thought I would surprise her."

A slight smile crept onto his face in apparent amusement. "Well, she probably has left for the day." He glanced at his watch. "Actually, the weekend. Would you like me to try to reach her on her cell phone?"

"Oh, that won't be necessary. I'll give her a call." As she pulled out her phone and dialed again, he continued.

"Do you have a reservation?"

Suddenly she felt rather awkward showing up unannounced. It was uncharacteristic of her—more like something Rashelle would have done. Her friend's phone rang on and on in her ear. She wasn't picking up.

"Is the inn open?" Searching his shirt pocket, she couldn't find a name tag. Who was she talking with? The night manager? A desk clerk?

"Yes. Well, about half of it. The goal was to complete renovations and open a week ago." He leaned forward as if speaking confidentially. "You know how construction goes. *Never* on schedule." His eyes twitched slightly. Had she hit a nerve? "Memorial Day weekend is the official start of the peak season, but we obviously didn't make it. There's the wedding here tomorrow—a small one—so I guess we had to open. We're only able to offer about half of the rooms. Even less of our cottages. They're still not complete."

"Cottages?" She didn't remember Rashelle mentioning anything about cottages in her description.

"Yes, studios and one-bedroom cottages located on the property behind the main building. They're rather quaint, actually." He seemed oddly proud of them. "Let me have a look. I should be able to find a place for you to stay the night, especially if you aren't able to catch up with your friend. Just give me a minute. This isn't my regular job so I'm still figuring it out. I wasn't expecting to be filling in tonight."

He busied himself at the computer screen on the reception desk. With the glow of the monitor, his face took on the look of an older, sinister-looking man. Elizabeth shook off the image, glancing around the lobby, hoping to catch sight of Rashelle. Hanging up, she reluctantly admitted she would have to spring for a room for the night.

After hitting a few strokes on the keypad, he took a swat at the monitor. "Oh, I can't get the darn thing to work. Didn't have a problem earlier, but now it's not cooperating. And no one else is here who might know more about it than I do to ask." Scanning below the counter, his frustration lightened. "Looks like we have a room in the East Wing. That portion of the building is still under renovation, but it should be quiet. Work isn't starting back up until Monday morning. You wouldn't mind staying there, would you?" Reaching to the side, he kept his eyes firmly glued to the computer screen, as if waiting for a response, up until his last two words when he looked up to her.

"Oh that would be fine. Thank you. I'm sorry to have caused you the inconvenience." She was genuinely grateful, yet feeling uncomfortable to be at his mercy.

His forced grin didn't match the unsure look in his eyes. "No problem at all, Miss Pennington. I can put you in 213. It's up on the second floor." He motioned toward the imposing staircase, leaning forward to hand her the key.

She was surprised to see it was an old-fashioned skeleton key, a scarce oddity in the world of technology. He got so close to her when he leaned over that she stepped back slightly, causing Buddy to stand up and step sideways. His tags jingled, which drew the attention of the night manager, reservation clerk, or whoever he was.

"Oh! . . . You've brought your pup with you." He sounded unsure how to handle a furry guest.

Elizabeth realized with a feeling of dread they might have a "no dog" policy.

He returned her gaze and held it, waiting for her to respond.

"I'm sorry . . . again. Dogs aren't allowed?" A sickening feeling crept into her stomach.

He hesitated. "Well, not entirely. From what I've been told, we usually put guests with dogs in one of the cottages, but renovations are complete in only two of them, and both are booked for the weekend." He shifted uncomfortably behind the counter.

"I'm sorry to put you on the spot like—"

"But I'm sure Mrs. Sterling wouldn't mind if I made an exception for a friend of Shelly's . . . just this once." He looked like he wanted to continue but clenched his teeth instead.

Shelly? Interesting they called her that. Elizabeth only referred to her as Rashelle or Shelle. No matter. She'd have to remember to tease her when she caught up with her. At the moment, she needed to grovel. "I'd really appreciate it. Thanks."

He extended his hand. "You're welcome, Miss Pennington. By the way, I'm Chip, the night manager—well, for tonight anyway. At least, I hope. Usually I'm a bellhop." He gestured toward the stand near the front doors.

"Well, Chip, great job," she attempted to encourage him but was disappointed such an inexperienced person was left to handle check-ins. First impressions were critical. Guests could decide early on if they expected to have a positive experience, even if the inn wasn't officially open yet.

"Thanks, ma'am. I appreciate that. Hope you enjoy your stay. Let us know if you need anything while you're with us."

"I will. Thank you very much."

"Good night."

"Good night." Elizabeth leaned down and picked up Buddy's leash and led him back through the lobby, leaving behind the rookie clerk. The cool night air felt good on her face. She tried Rashelle one more time as they walked back to her car.

Still no answer. Probably driving home. Or out at a bar. Busy talking. Something like that. She was starting to wonder if surprising Rashelle was such a good idea after all.

CHAPTER FIVE

Once she'd gathered their belongings, Elizabeth headed back through the lobby with Buddy close at her heels. Relieved to see no one behind the desk, she dropped the leash and Buddy scampered up the stairs with Elizabeth doing her best to catch up. At the top, she looked up and down the hallway. No one in sight and blissfully quiet. A small sign on the wall indicated Room 213 was located to the right.

As the night manager had mentioned, renovations were clearly still underway on the half of the floor where they would be staying. Scaffolding pushed up against the walls held commercial-sized buckets of paint left abandoned for the weekend. Drop cloths protecting the floor in the hall muffled their footfalls as they ambled from hardwood to carpet and back again. Elizabeth was careful to step around miscellaneous tools scattered along the way. Buddy had no problem trotting through the obstacle course. An errant smell caught his attention from time to time, but he could easily be brought back on track with an "uh-uh" from Elizabeth. Even though he was still a puppy, he was becoming a very well-behaved dog. She was so pleased he responded to the sound of her voice.

At the end of the hall they found the room on the left. She dropped a weekend bag and a tote on either side of her and pulled the intricate metal key out of her pocket. It felt fragile, almost brittle in her fingers, as though it would snap off in the lock. The dark wooden door with its polished brass placard that read "213" was like all the others they had walked by, but somehow it felt different to her. Since it was on the back side of the inn, it would have a view of the grounds in the rear. Elizabeth was anxious to see what they held.

With Buddy sitting at her feet, Elizabeth pushed the key into the lock and turned, hoping the door would open easily. To her dismay, it did not. She pulled it out, pushed it back in and turned again. The lock, displaying what she imagined was the temperament that comes with old age, wouldn't budge. Had he given her the wrong key? She tried once more, reluctant to head back down to the lobby too soon, looking like a helpless female needing assistance with such a simple task.

Suddenly aware of someone behind her, she turned to see a man who looked to be in his mid-twenties, dressed in a traditional bellman's uniform. It was dark blue with dull brass buttons and a matching flat brimless hat, a bit old-fashioned, but she admired the inn's effort to maintain tradition. She hadn't heard him approach and was startled to see him. Her furry friend sized up the unexpected visitor with a low growl and then sat down closer to Elizabeth, between her and the bellman.

"Are you going to be staying in this room tonight?"

Elizabeth, perplexed by his question, kept to the obvious. "Yes, I am."

There appeared to be something on his mind. "That's Miss Livingston's room. Are you a friend of hers?"

"Miss Livingston? Well, no, I . . . It will probably be just for the night, though," she tried to assure him and then re-focused her attention on unlocking the door with the antique key.

"It gives her trouble sometimes too." He chuckled softly. "Just be careful; those keys tend to open more than they were meant to."

A voice from down the hall called, "Miss Pennington." It was the bellman-turned-manager jogging toward her. "I'm sorry. I forgot to give you this." He held out a white piece of paper.

She took the single sheet, printed on both sides.

"It's recommendations for activities in the area as well as the shuttle bus schedule—although I think they're not sticking to the schedule yet, with so few people at the inn. I think it's more like they'll take you wherever you need to go, whenever you want to."

"Great to hear. Thanks."

As he left her to deal with the stubborn door, she slipped the key in again, unlocking number 213 with a click. Elizabeth, somewhat astonished it had finally worked, gave it a shove with her hip, and it groaned, wood against wood, to reveal a predominantly dark room. Moonlight illuminated the far side of it.

"Have a good evening," Chip called back to her.

"Thanks. You as well."

Through the open doorway, a cool, musty odor permeated the air as if a window had been left open. Buddy remained fixated on his spot. Reaching inside, she groped for the light switch, but her fingers didn't catch anything. She was going to have to venture farther into the room.

Glancing back to dismiss the bellman, she realized he was already gone, clearly having more important matters to attend to once Chip arrived on the scene. She stepped into the room, leaving the door open to make use of the hall light. Buddy remained on the threshold, his nose sniffing the air, unwilling to venture into the dark. Elizabeth crept along, arms flailing in front of her, groping for something to grab onto, hoping to find a table or floor lamp, whatever she could get her hands on first.

Elizabeth glanced back at Buddy sitting resolute, the hallway light carving a profile of his body. "Really, Bud? Could you gather a little more courage and come with me? I would love some help finding a light," she teased as if he was going to respond to her comments. "Fine, you stay there. I'll be the brave one." She chuckled at the notion he knew what she was saying.

Pushing her way through the darkness until her shin banged against a hard surface, she grabbed her leg, biting her lip. "Ugh!" She snatched a breath.

Her pup let out a whimper to let her know he was concerned, yet not brave enough to enter the unfamiliar dark space.

"I'm okay, Bud. Hang on. I'll find a light. . . . Good lord. So much for being a fearless companion," she murmured to herself.

Waving her arms over the obstruction, Elizabeth hoped to make contact with a lamp. None there. She redirected her route around the obstacle, shuffling several steps until she made contact with a lampshade. A few more seconds of groping and she found the switch. A click and the lamp illuminated a small portion of the room. Cut crystal knobs on an old dresser caught the light, inviting her to pull open the drawers to see what lay inside.

"Come on, Bud. Come on in," Elizabeth coaxed. Plodding across the room, he ambled into her open arms. "Atta boy!" She grabbed his head with both hands, nuzzling her face next to his and hugging his slender body. "I love you, big guy." She held her embrace and breathed in his scent. The bond between the two grew stronger every day.

He sat down at her feet and Elizabeth gave him a couple more solid pats on his sides but then focused on locating another light. Spying the outlines of lamps on either side of the bed, she closed the distance to the nearest one, reaching under the shade and turning the switch.

"Wow," she whispered to herself. As if to explain the musty smell that had greeted them, the furnishings looked like they hadn't been touched since the early part of the twentieth century. There was a Victorian feel to it. A dark four-poster bed positioned on a side wall and parallel to the door was the focal point of the room with its dusty mauve floral bedding and pillows piled high at the head. Step stools waited on either side to facilitate climbing up onto the high mattress. Bedside tables were former washbasin stands complete with antique pitchers and bowls sitting on top. Long, slender tapered candles in simple brass candlesticks stood next to the bowls as if they were, once, the only source of light.

As Elizabeth continued to take in the room lost in time, her eyes traveled along the intricate design of the wallpaper. It was an old-fashioned floral pattern, quite possibly original to the room and competed fiercely with the bedding for attention. She wrinkled her nose at a cobweb dangling from ornate crown moldings framing the top of the walls along the ceiling. Beneath her feet was a large rectangular floral rug that lay on top of a hardwood floor. A diminutive crystal chandelier hung from the center of the ceiling and caught the minimal light from the two lamps, sending off sparkling reflections throughout the room. She wondered if anyone had stayed there recently.

A tickle crept up her nose, and she shook her head, hoping to squelch the sneeze. It became uncontrollable, and finally she let out a delicate "phzew!" Two more sneezes followed in quick succession and then her trademark yawn to complete the sequence. From the shadows came a canine sneeze, one that jingled his tags. Elizabeth snickered. Apparently the power of suggestion worked on dogs, too.

Two sets of French doors lay open on the far wall. Grasping the oblong metal handles protruding in opposite directions, hard and cold to the touch, Elizabeth pushed one set closed and made her way over to the threshold of the other, stepping out onto a small Juliet balcony. The view below was breathtaking, looking very much like she would imagine a formal English garden. The moon cast a soft spotlight on the well-manicured bushes and plantings among walkways, urns, fountains, and a reflecting pool. From her vantage point, the backyard expanse looked to be at least an acre. Next to an open rectangular courtyard was a maze of twists, turns, sharp corners and dead ends. Suddenly she felt as though she needed to be down there.

Elizabeth turned back into the room and noticed Buddy sitting in the open doorway, framed by the two bags she had dropped earlier and looking as though he was packed and ready to leave. "Buddy!" His tail wagged at the sound of her voice. Clearly he didn't feel comfortable in the room and had retreated. It was time to go explore the grounds behind the house, let him stretch his legs a bit.

Sliding their bags into the room, she pulled out a fuzzy yellow tennis ball and shoved it into the pocket of her jacket. In a passing thought, she mused that one day she would actually buy balls to play tennis with, not just to throw for her furry friend. As they made their way down the hall, Elizabeth tried Rashelle's cell one more time. It rang until voicemail picked up. She decided to leave a message this time.

"Shelle, it's Lizzi. Hope everything is okay. I've been trying to reach you. Give me a call when you get this." Not wanting to give away the surprise, she stopped short of giving her any more information. It was Friday night. Rashelle was probably at a noisy bar and didn't hear her phone ringing. She'd try again later.

At the bottom of the stairs they made their way through the empty lobby and headed toward the back of the building, past an elevator marked "staff only" to a narrow hallway that led to a screened-in porch. The cool night air made her wish she'd thought to throw on a sweater under her light jacket. Their walk would need to be brief.

The porch ran the length of the house and had a wooden floor painted bright white. Oversized natural wicker chairs and loveseats with navy blue and white striped cushions were set up in conversation clusters. Toss pillows in a contrasting solid dusty red punctuated each seat. At the late hour, no one occupied any of the chairs or the white rockers outside on the patio.

A second door led from the porch to the gardens. Elizabeth pushed it and stepped off onto lush grass, wishing for a moment she was barefooted. Buddy was right behind her, anxious to get outside. She would have to do her best to keep an eye on him in the dark.

Buddy scampered to the far end of the yard, stopping randomly to sniff, looking like a true puppy exploring new territory. Not too far from where he was playing, there was something scurrying in the opposite direction. A rabbit, perhaps? Elizabeth quickened her pace to put less distance between herself and her pup. If he noticed the animal, she'd lose him for sure. His head popped up, and he looked in her direction, sensing she was getting near. When she got close enough to connect with him, she pulled the tennis ball from her pocket and showed it to him. He instinctively dropped into a playful stance, looking intently at the toy, his tail wagging furiously.

"Go get it!" She threw it past him, down a straight section of the path so he could follow where it went. Eagerly he tore after it, overshooting where it landed so he had to put on the brakes and backtrack to the fuzzy, yellow orb. Chomping down on it, he trotted back to her, his back end wiggling. She retrieved the soggy ball from his jaws and threw it again. He scampered after it, the spring in his step emulating the movement of the ball. Feeling a bit envious of his carefree life, Elizabeth kept the game going while she walked on the garden path. A small sign for Sandpiper and Sea Glass Cottages pointed down a narrow gravel path that disappeared into the woods. They seemed to be very private places to stay. She liked that idea.

Reaching the top edge of the yard, Elizabeth threw the ball again. As Buddy chased after it, the ball bounced, catching an edge of the slate, propelling it into the row of bushy pines lined up along the garden. She clenched her teeth, figuring that one was gone for good. Stopping in a lurch as if someone had tugged on his collar, Buddy turned to follow the ball and his nose went to the ground, moving from side to side in pursuit. Elizabeth laughed at how easily distracted he was. She wondered if dogs could be ADHD. Just as she started to jog toward him, Buddy dove into the greenery where the ball had disappeared.

Breaking into a dead run, she aimed for where he had slipped out of sight and came upon a set of wide stone stairs that didn't appear to have been used for a while. The pine trees had been allowed to encroach upon them and obliterated the landing at the top. She climbed the crumbling steps, pine needles tickling her arms.

"Buddy!" She couldn't see through the thick trees. "Buddy!" she called, desperately hoping he would hear her and return. "Buddy, come here!" She stood silently on the tips of her toes, listening, hoping his adorable face would poke back through the evergreens.

There was no jingle of his tags. She was afraid he was already too far to hear her voice.

Bending forward at the waist, she dove into the thick pines, evergreen needles scraping across her arms and legs, as if trying to hold her back. Branches snapped as she pushed. One strong bough hit her directly and stung her face as she plowed through. Flickering stars obstructed her view, but it only slowed her down.

"Buddy!" She broke through to the other side of the thick pines. The smell of sweet, sticky sap hung in the air. Silence. Not even the peepers were talking. The air was thick and damp. It was eerily quiet, but the full moon illuminated the grounds in front of her. She could make out stones scattered in a clearing. Long grass that hadn't been cared for in a while obscured the bottom half of most of them. Some of the stones were rounded on the top, others were straight across. A cemetery. Perhaps a family burial ground. A chill ran through her body. She took a couple steps closer and noticed some aging stones lying flat on the ground, partially hidden. Creeping toward them, she started to make out some of the engravings.

A vibration against her backside startled her. Slipping her slender fingers into her pocket, she pulled out her cell. The number wasn't familiar. It vibrated again. Could it be Rashelle? Perhaps her battery had died, and she was using a different phone. Just in case, she pressed the answer pad. Too late. She waited to see if there was a voicemail . . . nothing.

"Shelle! Come on. At least leave me a message, for God's sake!" Elizabeth began to lose her patience. Fatigue was setting in.

Clouds were gradually moving inland, partially obscuring what had been a bright moon. The cemetery grew darker. Elizabeth needed to find her pup and make her way back to the inn, but a name on one of the tombstones caught her attention. Livingston. The same name that was on the stone pillars framing the ends of the driveway. Leaning over, she brushed away a patch of stubborn moss and examined the engraved words. Abigail Livingston. 1889–1913.

"Only twenty-four years old. How sad." Elizabeth couldn't keep from speaking out loud to the old stones. Abigail wasn't much younger than her when she died. "Too young. Wonder what her story was," she whispered. Next to Abigail was another Livingston. Samuel. 1883–1957. On the other side was Beatrice Livingston. 1901–1923. Elizabeth, lost in her thoughts of how remarkably few details the stones contained, felt a nudge on her leg. She cried out and jumped back, pulling away. Looking down she saw her sweet furry friend had found his way back. Ecstatic, Elizabeth bent down to hug him and clipped the leash onto his collar.

As clouds drifted farther inland, robbing them of light to navigate, she planned to return to explore further. Tomorrow would be another day to find out more about the Livingston family and hopefully catch up with Rashelle. Intrigued by their find, she snapped a couple photos of the grave markers on her phone before they pushed their way through the thick pines and down the steps of the old family burial ground.

Reaching the rear of the carriage house, Buddy stopped short, tugging on his end of the leash, and went nose down to the large double doors, open only a crack. His strong snout shoved one to the side, making an opening wide enough for his slender body to dart through. Her palm burned when he yanked the lead out of her grasp.

"Oh, where are you going?" Elizabeth tried to follow him but couldn't fit through. "Buddy, come back here." She planted her feet to get better leverage and tried to slide one of the heavy wooden panels. It barely budged. "Buddy, come!" Shoving her backside up against the edge of the door, she inched it far enough for her to slip through. Fumbling for her phone to illuminate the large space, she had the terrifying feeling something or someone lurked in the shadows. Snapping on the phone light, she could make out Buddy's shape on the far side, nose to the ground. Dashing to him, she grabbed him by the collar, but he lay down with his nose glued to the dirt floor.

"Let's go," she commanded, yet he remained steadfast, not taking his eyes from the spot in the shadows. "Now!"

Having no interest in learning what was catching the pup's attention, she yanked him by the collar, dragging him toward the narrow opening she had entered through. He let out a yelp, resisting with each step, but she got him to the entrance and pushed his back end through. Slipping out behind him, she was relieved to reach the screened-in porch and pulled him inside. The knob of the door leading into the inn, however, stopped short of turning completely around. She tried again with more oomph, but the knob would not yield. Clearly the skeleton key to her room was not going to work in the lock. Peering inside she hoped to see someone milling about, but there didn't seem to be anyone around at the late hour. She knocked on the glass several times, but no one came into view. She didn't like how this was playing out.

They circled around to the front to try the main entrance, trudging through thick, dewy grass that made the bottom of her shoes slippery and her feet soggy. As they approached the portico, a dark, late-model sports car parked farther down the circular drive came to life and sped off. Elizabeth and Buddy reached the front doors, and she tried the knob. It turned but also wouldn't budge.

"For God's sake, what time does everyone go to sleep in this town?" Tired and frustrated, she pounded on one of the large wooden panels. No one responded. She pounded again, more earnestly. She had no desire to spend the evening outside. Her furry companion whined softly and nudged against her leg. "Come on!" There had been at least a skeleton crew on hand earlier, but no one appeared to be around at the late hour.

She pulled out her phone, searched for the number for the inn, and pressed the dial pad. It rang several times until finally there was a click and a pause and then a masculine voice who answered, "Thank you for calling The Inn on Boothbay Harbor. May I help you?" It sounded like Chip.

"I certainly hope so." Elizabeth did her best to rein in her anger. "I'm a guest, and I'm stuck outside the front door. Could you send someone to let me in, please?"

"Certainly, Miss Pennington. I'll be right there."

It seemed odd he recognized who she was when she hadn't mentioned her name. Pulling the flaps of her jacket tighter around her body, she waited for him to arrive, patting Buddy on the head, grateful for his company.

A click on the other side announced the arrival of the bellman who opened both doors wide and welcomed them into the lobby with an outstretched arm. He looked far too eager to have her arrive again.

"Thank you so much. I really appreciate it. I had no idea they would be locked so early." She hated that she'd been reduced to groveling again.

"Well, during the regular season, the doors would usually still be open at this hour, but given the small number of guests we have at the moment, we stuck to the off-season guidelines. Sorry for any inconvenience, Miss Pennington. We certainly didn't mean to leave you out in the dark."

Off-season versus regular season hours were none of her concern, and she really didn't care to get into a discussion about it. "Thanks for letting us in. We were out for a walk and didn't realize how late it had gotten."

"Glad I was here to help."

"Yes, thank you so much. I really appreciate it." She pushed past him with her pup in tow, tired of the superficial chitchat.

Eager to get to their room, she scampered up the grand stairs with her pup at her heels and made record time arriving at the doorstep of 213. Elizabeth inserted the skeleton key and this time very skillfully turned it and slipped into the musty-smelling murkiness. Only cloud-filtered moonlight spilled through the French doors. Elizabeth headed for the lamp she'd found earlier. Fumbling for the switch, she finally made contact but didn't recall turning it off before they had left. While Elizabeth quickly washed up, Buddy fidgeted outside the bathroom door.

Pulling down the covers on the imposing four-poster bed, she hastened inside, but Buddy didn't seem comfortable, pacing back and forth until Elizabeth scolded him and told him to lie down. He resigned himself to a spot beside the bed, letting out a cathartic exhale. Elizabeth responded in kind, wondering what the next day would bring. Suddenly she felt an uncontrollable urge to sneeze. She tried hard to hold it in but couldn't. A rather loud, abrupt "phzew" ripped through the still of the room, startling the pup. His tags jingled. She wiggled her nose, trying to dispel any lingering desire to sneeze again, then settled back down onto the pillow and yawned. She lay still and tried to will her body to relax. A canine sneeze in the dark made her smile. If they were going to stay in the room for the weekend, she would have to find the local drug store and pick up some antihistamine . . . for both of them.

CHAPTER SIX

Sleep wouldn't come. Shifting positions, unfurling the covers from around him only to wrap back up in them again, did little to improve his situation. Abandoning the god-awful excuse for a bed, he staked out a post at the windows with full view of the grounds and began to sway back and forth, like a mother trying to soothe a baby.

If only she hadn't made him so angry. She had unleashed something inside that terrified him. It was as if someone else was controlling his hands. He could only watch from deep within himself, unable to scream to let go. Back away. Now he just wanted her back.

No one could find out about his unthinkable act. Not even a suspicion. It would ruin everything. All he had worked so hard for. His thoughts traveled to the carriage house floor.

The packed dirt had proved unexpectedly hard. Decades of getting tamped down by wagon wheels and later by motorized vehicles left the surface nearly impenetrable. Digging had been arduous, and he wished he'd had other options to hide the body.

The section of the floor clearly appeared disturbed where he'd dug, in spite of his best efforts to make it look like it had before. It practically called out to whoever ventured near that something was amiss and should be investigated. He was desperate to solve his dilemma. Surely someone would ask about it. Then it hit him. All he had to do was to disturb the rest of the floor. Then it would be uniform. But would that look unusual? Would someone question it? Who would care?

Relieved he'd arrived at a solution, he wasted no time in heading back out to the carriage house while the inn and the town slept, snatching the rake from its hook and starting in the far corner. A few strokes in, he admonished himself for not thinking it through. Given the size of the floor, it could take more than one night to finish. But that wouldn't do. His dirty deed was there for everyone to see. Should he dig it up again and take it elsewhere? But where? He couldn't risk anyone noticing. Better to leave well enough alone.

Shoving a hand deep into his pocket, he pulled out his keys. Slipping them onto the first two fingers of his left hand, his gaze wandered to the carriage house door and the latch bolted securely from the inside as he twirled the ring effortlessly around. Once. Twice. Three times and then back in again.

With no better ideas presenting themselves, he resumed raking. It would be several hours before the light of dawn, at which time he would slip out quietly on one of the bikes.

CHAPTER SEVEN

Elizabeth *awoke to a tug* of the covers. Warm, moist breath accosted her face. She wrinkled her nose and turned over, away from the sour smell. Her eyelids were too heavy to open; her body ached from an unfamiliar mattress. Surely it was still early morning. Another tug on the covers. This time with a soft whimper. She opened one eye and could see daylight pouring in through the French doors. It might be later than she thought. Buddy's stomach and bladder were on a regular schedule, and it sounded as though it was time to take care of both.

"Ugh! Buddy, go lie down. It can't be time to get up yet." She swatted the air a few times with her hand and then let it flop back down on the bedding. Silence. Hoping that bought her a few more minutes, rather like a snooze button on an alarm clock, she started to doze off when she felt a more forceful tug. "Aaarrrruff!" He wasn't having any of her sleeping in.

"All right, all right!" Elizabeth resigned herself to the obvious fact she couldn't postpone the morning any longer. Kicking off the covers, she threw her legs over the side and slid off onto the floor. The bright morning light washed the entire room, infusing it with an energy it lacked the night before. Elizabeth paused to take it in, unable to shake the feeling she'd fallen asleep in the twenty-first century and woken up in the Victorian Era.

Fumbling through Buddy's bag, she found his food container and scooped a portion of dry kibbles into his dish. While he gobbled his breakfast, she showered and then grabbed a small drawstring bag, filling it with a couple water bottles, snacks, and other necessities for their day's outing.

After a romp around the backyard, they retraced their steps to the lobby. Elizabeth was pleased to find a long, narrow table set up with coffee and hot water urns and platters of breakfast breads and pastries.

An elderly couple entered the inn and crossed the grand foyer, holding hands and shuffling their feet like their legs were too tired to lift properly. He was bald with a band of short, thin, gray hair around the base of his head, connecting one ear to the other. She had thin white hair that had been meticulously pulled back into a neat bun. He was sporting dark pleated trousers pulled high above his waist, a light tan cardigan sweater, and dark dress shoes. She had on a medium-blue and white flowered cotton dress with a white scalloped-edged sweater and matching strappy summer sandals that revealed the reinforced toes of her support hosiery. Elizabeth thought the couple was absolutely adorable and was amused by the innocence they carried with each labored step.

The desk clerk looked up just before they reached her. "Well, hello! Welcome back, Mr. and Mrs.—!"

The elderly man held up a gnarled and crumpled hand to gently correct her. "Oh, now I told you on the phone to forget about protocol with us and call us by our first names, Floyd and Lee." The man released hands with his wife and extended his arm around her shoulder. "This isn't our first time here, ya know." All three joined in whimsical laughter.

As the couple continued with check-in, Elizabeth grabbed a cup of coffee and wrapped a croissant in a paper napkin. Buddy sat quietly at her side, waiting patiently for their jaunt into town. Boothbay with its quaint shops and restaurants lay across the harbor from them. She figured it would be a lengthy walk, but they could both use the exercise after the long ride up the night before.

A tall, handsome young man who looked young enough for this to be his first job stood proudly at a bellman's podium and glanced up as they approached. He was dressed much more casually than the gentleman who had stopped by the prior evening when she was struggling to get into her room. This bellman wore a green polo shirt with "The Inn on Boothbay Harbor" printed in bold white letters on the left side along with a pine tree logo. Perhaps they were still working out all the details of their reopening. Or it was simply a matter of summer versus off-season uniforms. Either way, his piercing cool blue eyes and blond tousled hair brought her attention away from the uniform discrepancy.

"Good morning, ma'am." He had a compassionate face that pulled her in, so she slowed her gait.

"Good morning." She echoed his warmth.

"Is there anything I can assist you with this morning?" He sounded far too eager.

Stopping to consider several possible answers to his question, she noticed a name plate on the right side of his shirt that read, "Owen."

Resting his forearms on top of the podium, he leaned toward her, revealing deep dimples; his arms and neck were a luscious dark tan from the sun. Bulging muscles on his upper arms stretched the hems of the short-sleeved shirt. Elizabeth pictured him out sailing in the harbor, perhaps venturing out into the ocean on his days off. His nose appeared painfully red as if a layer of skin had been sunburned and then peeled off to reveal a newer, more sensitive layer.

He glanced down at her companion. "What a nice-looking fellow you've got there." He walked out from behind the podium, bent down, and extended his hand for Buddy to sniff before he petted his head. He wore light-colored khakis and dark brown boat shoes, looking like he had just stepped off the sailboat she'd been envisioning.

"Yes, well, thank you very much. He's a real sweetheart." Funny, he didn't think it was odd to see a dog at the inn.

"My parents have a couple of Labs. I grew up with them. They're such great dogs. Very loyal, rather mellow, go with the flow." Owen stroked Buddy's back and sides so he sat there, enjoying the attention, very comfortable with the new stranger who suddenly leaned back on his heels. "Oh! I'm probably holding you up, aren't I? I'm sorry." He stood up and retreated to the stand. "I couldn't resist saying hello."

"No worries at all. I would have done the same thing." She tried to ease his mind a bit. Chances were, he was new to the job, perhaps feeling self-conscious he was being observed and critiqued while he worked.

Owen headed back around the other side of the podium. "So, is there anything I could help you with this morning?" he tried again.

"I don't think so. . . . We were going to head into town. Any place you can recommend for lunch?" Even though that wasn't really a bellman's area of expertise, she was interested in what his answer would be.

"Certainly! There are several options and, of course, it will depend upon what you're looking for." He dove into the back of the podium and pulled out a colorful map of Boothbay Harbor, unfolding it and placing it on top. Launching into a short dissertation of his favorite restaurants, he circled a couple lunch options, giving a brief description of each one.

She interrupted him. "Where would *you* go?"

Owen looked up from the map. "That's easy. A place called Chauncey's. It's casual. Food's great, and they have a nice assortment of craft beers—that is, if you're into that. They have a great wine selection, too, especially for a relatively small place. It's really good, though. I think you'd like it."

Pleased to be armed with his recommendations, Elizabeth took the map and thanked him for his help. He wished them well on their way out.

A white minibus was parked directly across from the front steps under the portico. The inn's name and pine tree logo were emblazoned in dark green on the side under a row of windows. An older, African American man wearing a green polo shirt like the bellman's was leaning up against the bus. His arms were folded and resting comfortably onto his rather large, round protruding belly. His closely trimmed brown hair was peppered with silver, and his pearly whites gleamed.

"Good morning, ma'am! Can I give you a lift somewhere?" He was also overly perky for a Saturday morning.

"Good morning." Leaning over to Buddy, she stroked his head. "Thank you, but we were going to walk into town."

He whistled through his clenched teeth and chuckled. "Well, aren't you two ambitious!" His broad grin remained firmly planted on his face, quite comfortable there. His eyes joined in, too.

Elizabeth paused to consider his reaction. "How far is it?"

"Well it depends on where, exactly, you're heading, but it's a good couple of miles just to get to the beginning of the loop. Of course, the footbridge will probably save you three-quarters of a mile."

The mere mention of the pedestrian footbridge brought back memories of skipping across the wooden planks with her grandmother trying to keep up. It cut across at the head of the harbor and boasted a small structure in the middle of the span that, over the years, had been used as a residence, a fish market, and an art gallery. Elizabeth always thought it would be an interesting place to live, perched over the water, particularly in the summer months, but at the expense of one's privacy.

"Oh, well, it's such a beautiful morning; I think we'll hoof it. I'm not in any particular hurry. Besides, is he even allowed on the bus?" She patted Buddy's head. He looked up at her in admiration and obediently sat down at her side.

"Well . . . technically, no." He took a few steps closer to her and lowered his voice. "But I don't seem to have anyone else to transport at the moment, and he looks like a well-behaved guy." There was a twinkle in his eye as he glanced down at her pup.

"Thank you, he really is, and that's very kind of you, but I wouldn't want you to get into any trouble over us. We'll walk."

"Okay, ma'am. You suit yourself, but at least take my card so you have my number in case you change your mind for the walk back. I'm Lorenzo." He quickly slipped a white business card out of his shirt pocket and handed it to her. "You have a good day now," he offered.

Elizabeth took the card and secured it in her back pocket. "Thanks, Lorenzo. I appreciate it."

"Call me if you want a ride, I'll come get you," he called after them.

Elizabeth turned back and thanked him one final time. He seemed sweet. Probably dreadfully bored. Not very many guests to be transporting.

Partway down the walkway toward the harbor, she paused to survey the property spread out in front of her in the bright sunshine and enticingly seductive sea air. Instinctively, Buddy stopped in his tracks, waiting for a signal from her. Elizabeth remembered Rashelle saying something about the inn not being very close to the water. She acknowledged that the expansive yard in front of the mansion was quite grand, but the harbor was just beyond the road and a small strip of land with a dock. The rooms on the second floor that faced that direction must enjoy stunning views. She resumed her pace with Buddy trotting happily next to her.

With the strong sun and a cool breeze off the water, the day was turning out to be a spectacular one.

At the edge of the road that ran along the water, they crossed to the other side so they'd be walking against traffic. With no sidewalk, Elizabeth hung on tightly to Buddy's leash and tried to move off to the side as much as they could when they encountered oncoming cars. It wasn't a terribly busy road, but drivers went much faster than the posted speed limit. Certainly much faster than was necessary. After all, they were in Maine. *What could possibly require them to be in such a hurry?*

The first car that whooshed past startled Elizabeth and stirred up sand and small pebbles, spraying them onto the pair. She switched the leash to her left hand and guided Buddy over, away from the active roadway. Another car approached, but she was relieved to see it slowed when it neared. They pressed on, Buddy trotting along happily and Elizabeth walking at a brisk clip. A couple cars approached from behind them, heading toward town. A gentle burst of air brushed against them after each car passed. Elizabeth began to question her decision to walk.

Sunlight sparkling on the calm water, disturbed only by an occasional boat slowly making its way out of the harbor, was mesmerizing. Lobster fishermen would have already headed out to check their traps; they got an early start. So it was pleasure crafts traveling in the opposite direction as them.

A large sailboat with a couple of bikini-clad bathing beauties slipped by without a sound. Three novice kayakers struggled to navigate through small wakes created by the other boats. Buddy was oblivious. His nose was directed forward, veering only to sniff an interesting scent as he passed but never interrupting his gait. More cars rumbled past, in both directions, each time pulling her attention away from the views of the harbor. Were they halfway to the footbridge yet? She wondered if it made sense to head back and take Lorenzo up on his offer when she sensed a large vehicle approaching from behind.

The minibus from the inn. It slowed to a stop with a squeak of the brakes. The driver's side window slid open and an animated Lorenzo stuck his head out, his face beaming, exuding positive energy.

"Thought I'd better come see how you two were doing. I was thinking you might be having second thoughts and want to get a ride so you could conserve your energy for shopping." He chuckled at his own humor.

His bubbly demeanor tickled her. "Oh, Lorenzo. You're too sweet. That's very kind of you," she called over. Acknowledging the walk was more treacherous and much longer than she'd expected, she was thrilled he'd come after them but felt the need to press him again. "I really wouldn't want you to get into trouble."

"Nonsense! Hop on and I'll whisk you into town and be back before anyone knows I'm gone." He motioned for them to cross the road.

Elizabeth glanced both ways, letting a car pass before she guided Buddy to the bus. The rattle of the door retracting frightened him, but with encouragement, he hopped up the steep steps, pausing at the top so he could give Lorenzo the sniff test and get his head patted. Elizabeth sat down on a bench seat to the left that ran parallel to the side of the vehicle so she was able to chat with their new friend. Buddy lay down at her feet, already hot and panting. Vowing to give him some water once they arrived in town, she patted his side and assured him softly.

"You picked a great time to visit the Boothbay Region." Lorenzo sat erect in his driver's seat, bouncing as if to music only he could hear. "A lot going on downtown this weekend."

That translated to crowds and traffic for Elizabeth. Even more than the usual congestion for a summer weekend.

"We're celebrating Victorian Days. There's a sidewalk sale going on. You'll see lots of shops will have tables set up out front with special sales."

Elizabeth struggled to keep herself from frowning. The sidewalks weren't all that wide to begin with.

"And there are people from the historical society dressed in period costumes that you'll see. There are kayak races in the harbor. They start at the pedestrian bridge and go out around Tumbler Island and back again. I think there's a shorter loop for younger kids that goes out around McFarland Island. And old-fashioned games out on a lawn somewhere. One of the inns? I don't really remember. But you could ask around. Someone local should know. I think there's croquet and marbles, and what's that game called where you have a wooden hoop and you're trying to keep it rolling with a stick?" He didn't wait for an answer. "Oh well, whatever, you know what I mean. . . . And let's see, what else. . . . The library is having a used book sale, and I think there are a couple authors doing book signings there. And there's got to be a farmers market around, too. Something for everyone!"

Lorenzo was obviously a proud ambassador to the area. Elizabeth admired him for that. "Wow, I had no idea when I decided to come up that I would have so much to choose from!" She genuinely tried to join in his enthusiasm. It would certainly be more fun if she could catch up with Rashelle.

"Aren't you just the luckiest gal in town," he gushed back at them and chuckled.

Through the front windshield, Elizabeth spotted the giant statue of a Maine fisherman in yellow rain gear standing outside Brown's Wharf on the left. That meant they were getting close to the bridge.

"So you mentioned volunteers from the historical society—"

"Yes! Yes! You won't miss them. They'll have Victorian costumes on."

"And can you tell me where the historical society is located?"

"Absolutely! I can do even better than that." He sat up straighter at the thought. "We're going to be going right by it. It's at the beginning of the loop that I do through town."

"That's great. I would love to stop in and find out more about the area."

"If you want, I can drop you right at the doorstep."

"Oh, that would be wonderful. Thanks."

"Gonna' do a little digging?" He looked to her for more details.

"Yeah, I think it's so interesting to find out as much as possible about an area while I'm visiting." She allowed a crooked smile. "I bet there's a lot I could uncover about the inn's past."

Lorenzo turned toward her again, this time with a solemn expression, as if trying to search within her for her motives. He returned his focus to driving, looking straight ahead, and got suddenly quiet. A stop sign at the end of the road brought them to a halt near the top of the loop.

They watched several cars pass by on the one-way street heading out of town. Finally Lorenzo could turn right onto Townsend Avenue to begin the loop. After a few hundred feet, they had reached the top where they turned left onto Oak Street. Before long they were pulling up to the front of a modest Victorian-style structure on the right. White clapboard with black shutters. Formerly someone's home, the sign out front read "Boothbay Harbor Region Historical Society." A woman stood out front on the steps as if she'd been expecting Elizabeth and was waiting to greet her. She looked to be in her mid-sixties and was dressed in an exquisite burgundy dress with a high collar, long sleeves, and layers of ruffles toward the bottom of the long, poufy skirt. Elizabeth imagined it had a bustle in the back as well. A matching wide-brimmed hat completed her costume. Quite elaborate.

Lorenzo put the van in park, engaged the flashers and then turned toward her as she got up to exit, her bag of necessities in one hand, Buddy's leash in the other. She stopped when she saw his face still held a serious expression.

"Now, ma'am, let me give you a piece of friendly advice. You seem like a sweet lady, and I wouldn't want you to stir up any trouble by digging into something that was meant to be kept private."

"I . . . uh . . . I'm not sure what you mean." She didn't really care for his condescending attitude.

He shook his head slightly. "Just be careful where you look and how far you push, okay? Trust me."

CHAPTER SEVEN

Leaving it at that, she thanked him for the ride, and he reminded her to call him for a ride back. Their budding relationship had turned cold. The twosome headed down the steps of the bus and up the short sidewalk toward the house.

Clasping her hands together, chest high, the Victorian lady was clearly delighted to have visitors; one arm lifted slowly with her hand waving sideways at them like a beauty queen on a parade float.

"Well good morning, dear! Thanks for stopping by." She descended the couple of steps to meet them partway down the walk. Buddy sat obediently at Elizabeth's feet as soon as she stopped moving. The volunteer, whose handwritten name tag Elizabeth couldn't read, bent over and brusquely patted his head as if she was required to, but didn't really enjoy it. Turning her attention back to Elizabeth, she asked what brought them to the historical society.

Beads of perspiration painted an uneven sheen across her forehead. The summer heat along with the heavy fabric of her costume must have bordered on unbearable. And it was only mid-morning.

"Well, we're only here for the weekend, and I always like to learn about the places I visit. In particular, I would love to know more about the old inn where we're staying." Lorenzo's warning echoed in her mind, but she dismissed it.

"Oh, certainly!" Gathering up the bottom of her dress, she waved for them to follow her. Over her shoulder, she asked where they were staying.

"The Inn on Boothbay Harbor."

Stopping short on the second step, she threw up a gnarled hand to halt everyone behind her. She whirled partway around, grasping the narrow wrought iron railing to steady herself, her shoulders dropped ever so slightly. "How lovely. . . . I'm sorry, but he can't come inside." Her slender but crooked index finger pointed at Buddy who wagged his tail as if to plead. "We don't allow dogs."

Disappointed, Elizabeth allowed her face to fall, yet she understood. "No problem. I need to give him some water anyway. I'll just hook his leash to the bottom of the railing."

Once Buddy was secured and lapping his water in the shade of the mature bushes lining the front of the house, the two women representing two very different eras entered the historical society on a mission. Feeling a twinge of guilt leaving her furry friend behind, Elizabeth planned to make her visit brief.

Stale warm air hit her in the face as they entered, not the respite from the summer heat she was hoping for. The vestibule was tight with a steep narrow stairway leading up to the second floor and was painted a stark cool white, making it feel more like the museum it currently was than the home it had been originally. Only the dark brown banister and the dark frames on old sepia photos lining the walls provided relief from the lack of color. Rooms on either side were painted in the same shade of white and held an array of artifacts but were bereft of visitors. The Victorian lady walked briskly through the abbreviated hallway to the left of the stairs, making small talk over her shoulder, into a cramped room used as an office.

"I'm so glad you stopped by," she gushed with a flip of her hand, sounding a bit giddy.

"We're very proud of our society. The Boothbay Region Historical Society serves Boothbay, Boothbay Harbor, and Southport Island."

She tapped the tips of three fingers on one hand with the index finger from the other as she listed the towns. "Although Southport Island does have its own historical society," she added as an aside.

As a local, Elizabeth was surprised to learn Boothbay was a separate town from Boothbay Harbor. She had always referred to the whole area as Boothbay.

"I don't know how much you'll find on the inn, but I can certainly point you in a direction to look. We do have birth records, marriage records, death records. Might take a little digging. We'll find it, if it's here. A lot has to be done manually, but let's take a look at what we can find online first."

Elizabeth nearly ran into a bank of old metal file cabinets on the left wall as she entered the small office. Rusty dents suggested years of use, perhaps abuse; a couple drawers weren't quite closed, and papers stuck out through the narrow openings. Two mismatched desks with a narrow table separating them filled the center of the room. Each was loaded down with a large boxy computer monitor. The office had an antiquated feel, fitting for a historical society, but Elizabeth hoped this wasn't going to turn into an all-day affair to dig up something interesting. She still had a wedding to make an appearance at.

The Victorian lady clutched the back of the closer ergonomically correct chair, claiming it as her own. In one swift movement, she rolled it out and plopped down while removing her fancy hat, dropping it on top of the monitor. Her thin wispy brown hair, with a root line of gray, had a band around it where her hat had been. An odor of perspiration permeated the close space.

Elizabeth took the seat next to her, eager to dig in. "Well, I know the name that is etched into the old pillars at the end of the driveway is Livingston."

"Yes, dear, the Livingstons have owned the property for generations . . . until fairly recently, that is." Her name tag came into view and read "Florence."

The volunteer noticed where Elizabeth's eyes had landed. "Oh, pardon me. Where are my manners? I'm Florence, but you can call me Flo." She offered a limp hand that Elizabeth took hold of and regretted once she touched her sweaty palm.

"Elizabeth." She brought her back to the topic. "So, who's the owner now?"

"The last name is Sterling." She didn't look up from the computer screen. Her fingers danced across the keyboard.

"So when did the Sterlings purchase it?"

She looked up, but her eyes became fixated on a random spot on the ceiling as she pondered the question. "It wasn't actually purchased."

Elizabeth waited for her to continue. There was certainly more to the story.

Flo dropped her head, pausing as if trepidatious about continuing. "Lucretia Livingston grew up there. She was an only child. So when her parents passed away a few years ago and the estate was left to her—"

"She lost both parents? At the same time?" Elizabeth felt compelled to interrupt.

"Yes, it was so sad. Young Lucretia was away at college when it happened. It was late one winter during—I think it was the last semester of her senior year."

"What happened?"

"Carbon monoxide poisoning. The coroner and the police ruled it accidental."

"Do you think it was . . . accidental?"

Flo swallowed hard and shifted in her chair. "Let me just say there are those who have reason to doubt the findings."

"Do *you*?" Elizabeth pushed further.

"Well, there has been talk that their groundskeeper hadn't been hired too long before the accident." Her last word she put into air quotes. "Seemed to up and disappear right afterwards." The Victorian lady let that possibility hang in the air for a moment.

"Did you know them?"

"Oh, yes. Miranda, Lucretia's mother, was a friend of mine. . . . A *dear* friend of mine." Her voice faltered as her eyes welled. "It was devastating to lose her. I still can't believe they're gone. It was such a tragedy. This town isn't the same without them. They gave so much of themselves."

Gathering herself with a swipe of her eyes, she continued, firmly placing the focus back onto the unfortunate couple's daughter.

"Poor Lucretia. She returned home, never finished college, and tried to carry on without her parents who she'd been very close to. I imagine it was an incredible undertaking to keep the mansion going. Maintenance costs alone had to be astronomical. I'm sure her parents left her comfortable financially, but she must have recognized she couldn't maintain the place forever, living in it alone. She may have been burning through her funds too quickly, but I'm sure she couldn't bear to sell the place, either. It was the only home she'd ever known. So she decided to turn it into an inn. There has always been a tourist trade in Boothbay Harbor, so she just had to cross her fingers that the market could handle one more inn. A large one at that."

"It's such a beautiful mansion. So much larger than anything else in town. Her family must have done well."

"Yes, her grandfather built the house. He made his money in building sailing ships. Her father took over the business and became quite successful in his own right, expanding into selling supplies and provisions to fishermen. The ship building company at the south end of town is what was left after Lucretia's father sold off parts of the business."

Elizabeth listened with great interest. The society volunteer paused long enough for her to interject a question.

"So what's happened since Lucretia turned her home into an inn?" There had to be more, but she wondered how much she would be able to learn, being an outsider.

Florence looked as though she was trying to choose her words carefully, clenching her jaw and then relaxing it. "Lucretia met Jonathon Sterling, and apparently it was love at first sight. They married very quickly. Well—" She stopped and shook her head slightly, perhaps editing out her personal opinion, and then started again. "They married not long after she opened the inn. He's from England and travels a lot on business trips abroad, leaving Ms. Livingston alone for long periods of time. I'm not sure what sort of business he's in. . . . It may be antiques. Something like that. Some people think Mr. Sterling doesn't always agree with how she runs the inn, but that's not the opinion of the historical society, and there I go, getting off on a tangent." She laughed nervously and took a playful swat at Elizabeth's arm.

The silence that lingered seemed to prompt Flo to continue. "Have you met Mrs. Sterling?"

"No, I just got here last night and haven't seen her yet."

"Oh, she's quite lovely, inside and out. Everyone loves her. And you'll know her when you see her. She's got the most gorgeous long and wavy, flaming red hair. You would think she'd have a temper to match, but she doesn't. Sterling certainly does, but—" She clasped her frail hands so tightly, they turned white. "So they've reopened?"

"Yes, but only partially. More of a soft opening until all the renovations are complete. I think they kind of had to. There's a wedding there this afternoon."

"I see. . . . Well, that's the history of the inn in the last few years. And honestly, that last part was off the record, so to speak. You wouldn't find any of this documented here, except the marriage record." The volunteer's voice trailed off. "But you probably want to know more about the earlier history, don't you? That, I can help you with."

Pleased to have learned at least some of the current history, Elizabeth welcomed the chance to dig further. "Sure, that would be great. I actually stumbled upon an old cemetery beyond the gardens of the inn." She reached into her pocket and pulled out her cell. "I grabbed a couple photos while I was there." She tapped the face a few times, slid her fingers across and then held it out for Flo to see.

"Oh, this is fascinating. I didn't know there was a cemetery there." She clutched the phone with frail hands.

"It's quite overgrown and obviously not well taken care of. Definitely a family cemetery," Elizabeth pointed out.

Flo's hands began to quiver as she examined the photos. "Abigail Livingston. 1889-1913. Samuel. 1883-1957. And Beatrice. This is great. Let me write this down. I can verify if our records include these people and their dates."

"Do you have an email address? I can just send the photos to you attached to an email." Remembering she'd left Buddy tied up out front, she grew uncomfortable with how time had gotten away from them. "You know, I should really get going. I've left my pup alone for too long as it is."

"Oh, certainly. And you know, email is never my first instinct!" She chuckled at herself and then shared the society's email address.

Elizabeth forwarded the photos and hurried toward the exit. She turned back and realized Florence was right at her heels, hat tightly grasped in her fingers.

"Thank you so much for your help. I really appreciate it. I'll check in another time." Before she could step through the doorway, Elizabeth felt a strong grip on her forearm.

"Please don't pass along the very private information I shared with you about the Sterlings. I'm a new volunteer here, and I probably shouldn't have divulged all of that, particularly on a local family that's still living—Well, I don't know if I would call him local. . . ." She became distracted by her thoughts and loosened her grip on Elizabeth. "I certainly wish them the best."

"No problem. I'm looking forward to learning more about the Livingston family from years ago," Elizabeth assured her, trying to redirect her onto a more comfortable topic.

"Terrific, dear. I'll do some digging for you and see what I can come up with." She plopped her oversized hat on the top of her head and escorted her visitor across the threshold.

Anxious to rejoin Buddy and continue their day together, Elizabeth reached the bottom of the stairs where she'd tied his leash and let out a high-pitched shriek.

CHAPTER EIGHT

Buddy *was not where* she'd left him. His bowl of water was still next to the bush, and Elizabeth's drawstring bag was lying nearby. But no Buddy. Not even his leash.

"Oh my God, where could he be?" She scanned the yard. "Buddy, here boy!" Frantically she ran toward the sidewalk, looking up and down, pushing aside images of him crossing the busy street. She ran back toward the house, glancing under the bushes, lamenting her decision to leave him outside. Why had she left him alone, tied to the railing? She felt so selfish, desperately hoping he was all right.

"He must be around here somewhere." Flo was strikingly calm about the situation. Elizabeth couldn't stand the thought someone might not be as urgently searching for her pup as she was. A wave of nausea hit her in the gut. *What had she done?* She called his name repeatedly as she circled the Victorian home, hoping he was just sniffing the grounds and got carried away by a particularly interesting scent. Had he wandered farther, beyond the sound of her voice?

Had someone taken him? As her eyes brimmed, a single drop escaped and trickled down her cheek. She brushed it aside without really giving it much notice. How could anyone do such a thing? Time to expand the search area. She ran to the front, back down the walkway to the sidewalk. Again she scanned up and down the street, calling his name. No response. No sweet black furry face and wagging tail. Decision time. Left or right?

"Where do you think he could have gone, dear?" Flo had reappeared. Elizabeth spun around and took hold of her arm.

"I don't know! Please help me," she urged.

"Of course, dear," she assured with much less sense of urgency than her own.

"You head up the sidewalk." Elizabeth motioned with her hand. "I'll head toward the center of town."

"Okay, dear. Good luck."

They parted ways with Elizabeth dashing down the sidewalk. She broke into a jog, head swiveling back and forth to scan both sides of the street, calling Buddy's name. Families walking on the other side glanced over when she yelled. Her heart pounded. She reached the first cross street and stopped. Approaching the corner from the opposite direction was a lady dressed in a faded pink floral Victorian dress, less like a costume and more like clothes she was accustomed to wearing; a high ruffled neck, small buttons running down the front to the waist, a long skirt with a single ruffle at the bottom, and long sleeves that came to a point on the back of her pale hands. Unlike the volunteer at the historical society, she was not wearing a wide-brimmed hat.

It took a moment to comprehend what she was looking at. Next to the elderly woman was a handsome, black Lab mix trotting along as if he always took walks with his current companion, dragging his royal blue leash beside him down the sidewalk, heading straight toward her.

She stepped off the curb but then thought better of having a rendezvous in the middle of the street. He wagged his tail exuberantly, bolting toward Elizabeth. "Buddy!" She hugged him tightly, so grateful he'd returned. His back half nearly wiggled out of her grasp. He planted warm wet kisses on the side of her face, nose, and ear, wherever he could make contact. He was as happy to be reunited with her as she was with him.

"I am *so* sorry, Bud. I was so scared I had lost you forever. I'm so sorry." She hugged him tightly.

With his rescuer standing awkwardly next to them, almost intruding on their private moment, Elizabeth snatched the leash and stood up to speak to her. "Thank you so much for finding him. Where was he?"

"So this is your dog?" She did not address her question. Was she questioning their relationship?

"Yes! I can't imagine how he got away, but I was absolutely a mess when I realized he was gone. Thank you so much."

"Glad to be able to help and it was a happy ending."

"I can't thank you enough." Buddy sat at her feet, leaning into her legs, looking up at her.

"So are you visiting the area?"

"Yes, we're here for the weekend."

"Oh, how nice. And where are you staying?"

"The Inn on Boothbay Harbor."

The old woman's eyes flickered ever so slightly. Her pleasant expression disappeared, and she turned serious. "Oh dear." Her words were barely audible. "Bad things have happened there."

Elizabeth stepped closer, waiting to see if she was going to elaborate.

The woman leaned in and took Elizabeth's hands. Hers were cold to the touch. She didn't seem to be perspiring. Elizabeth desperately wanted to let go but felt trapped. The old woman held her stern gaze. "You need to be careful, young lady." She tightened her grip.

"Bad things," Elizabeth repeated. Her mouth was dry. Hardly able to get the words out, she tried to force a nervous smile she didn't feel.

"Yes, things have been swept under the rug there that no one knows about." Her brows narrowed as she considered the danger Elizabeth was in. "You need to get out of there," she implored. "Heed my warning." Pulling a hand free from their grip, she held up one bent finger and shook it for emphasis before returning it to Elizabeth's hands.

Frightened, Elizabeth took a step away. *Leave? Where was she going to go?* "Okay, I'll be careful." *Was the woman referring to the death of Lucretia's parents? Or something more recent? Were the guests in danger?* "We'll be fine. Thank you, though." Pulling her hands out of her tight grasp, Elizabeth yearned to be on her way. She was grateful for getting Buddy back but was troubled by the serious look in the woman's eyes and the urgent tone of her voice. Elizabeth tugged on his leash, and he was more than happy to start trotting along next to her. They crossed the street to put some distance between them and the old woman. "Bye . . . and thank you again," she called over her shoulder.

Once on the other side, Elizabeth glanced back, almost expecting the flowered lady to be on their heels after her stern warning. Relieved she was nowhere in sight, Elizabeth placed a quick call to the historical society, to let Florence know she could call off her search, and set her sights for the wharf in town where the hub of activity took place.

They zigzagged their way through tourists trudging along, in no discernible hurry, pushing baby strollers and walking small dogs with short legs who already seemed to have their fill of being on the other end of a leash. Once past the post office, they stumbled onto the bellman's recommendation—a quaint corner pub with a modest exterior. A beat-up lavender girl's bike leaned up against a sandwich board sign out front that listed the specials. Before she could read the list, a stocky six-foot or so guy stepped out of the bar and leaned up against the doorframe with his arms crossed and one foot kicked back. His dirty-blond, wavy hair was pushed to one side and his gentle smile beckoned her closer. She was drawn in like she hadn't been in a while.

His jeans were faded, but there were no holes in either knee. The straight legs covered all but the bottoms of cowboy boots.

He looked older than her, probably mid-thirties. As she got closer, she could see his eyes were a stunning blue, and they were fixed on her crossing the street.

"Come on, Bud. Let's go see what's up." He wagged his tail in response.

"Good morning!"

Almost expecting him to shout, "Howdy," she was struck by how much he looked out of place in a small harbor town in Maine.

Elizabeth could feel her face flushing. "Good morning."

"Welcome to Chauncey's Pub," he greeted her with a flourish of his hands.

He didn't exactly look like he fit in an Irish pub, either, but Elizabeth endeavored to keep an open mind.

"Can I interest you in a bite to eat? At least a beverage on a hot day like today. A frosty pint?" His eyes traveled down to her furry companion. "He can come in, too. I've got a dog dish with water if he's thirsty." He gestured to a bowl just inside the entrance.

Pleased he'd made accommodations for canines, she couldn't shake the feeling he reminded her of someone in her not-too-distant past. There was an odd twinge in her gut as she felt herself getting swept away like the sand on a beach during a hurricane. She struggled to rein in her infatuation yet enjoyed being pulled in by his boyish charm.

Following the two into the pub, he headed behind a long wooden bar with a commanding presence. Rows of hard alcohol bottles were lined up in front of a large rectangular mirror with the pub's logo painted at the top in bright greens and yellow with a caricature-like leprechaun winking under a top hat. Built-in shelving ran along both sides of the mirror and held an array of different-shaped glasses. The cabinetry beneath it provided closed storage and housed two small beverage refrigerators with clear glass doors. Chauncey's had a decidedly masculine feel to it with its dark wood and dim lighting. Sunshine spilling in the front windows along the sidewalk provided some relief.

Elizabeth slid up onto the black leather seat of a stool with a curved back. Buddy lay down on the floor at her feet. Behind her were eight to ten square tables dispersed throughout the room, and booths lined the front and side windows. A handful were occupied.

"What can I get you?" the friendly bartender asked with high hopes, leaning in close with his forearms resting on the edge of the bar.

"I didn't catch your name," she playfully tossed back his way, a tingle rippling through her abdomen.

A smirk spread slowly across his face as if amused. "It's Ben."

"Ben, nice to meet you. Elizabeth." She extended her hand and laughed as they shook awkwardly. His hand was warm, strong, yet gentle in hers. "I'll just have a mimosa for now. It's not anywhere near lunch time."

"A mimosa, it is," he announced and turned to fill her order.

Having a second thought, she caught him as he grabbed a bottle of orange juice. "Oh, wait. Can you make that a peach Bellini?"

Tilting his head, studying her more closely, he grinned again, then nodded. "Sure, I can do that."

As he prepared her drink she let her mind wander and her eyes travel around the room. She imagined the Victorian Days' festivities had a hand in filling most of the seats in the bar that were taken and looked to include a few locals as well. A lone waitress chatted with a couple near the front windows.

Before long, the Bellini arrived in a fluted glass with a raspberry and mint leaf garnish on top. Ben launched into what was probably his standard bartender banter.

"So where ya from?"

"At the moment, Connecticut."

"Ah, and what's your dog's name?"

"Oh, that's Buddy."

"Looks like he might be a good hunter."

Chuckling at his suggestion, Elizabeth countered, "Hunter? No. He does have a great nose, but I don't think he'd make much of a hunter. He only got partway through his training as a search and rescue dog before he flunked out. Didn't have the right temperament, too docile. They need dogs with lots of energy to do that kind of work. Lucky for me, I got to adopt him."

"Nice."

"Do you hunt?" It was certainly possible, given that he lived in Maine. A lot of people hunted there.

"Nah. I'm more of a cowboy. Grew up in Montana. Learned to rope before I could ride a bike."

"How did you end up on the East Coast?"

He hesitated. "I came to connect with family."

She acknowledged with a nod.

"So where are you staying?" Grabbing a white dish towel and a large beer stein that had been left to drip on the side of the divided sink, he began drying a variety of glassware, holding up each one to the limited light for inspection before inserting it onto the shelf behind him.

"Over at The Inn on Boothbay Harbor." She motioned with her head in the general direction she thought the inn was located across the harbor.

His hands froze momentarily. "I see. And how do you like it there?"

"Oh, it's quite lovely. The setting, looking out over the harbor, is absolutely stunning."

"Didn't realize they'd reopened." His jaw clenched, and his eyes took on a dangerous look, the precursor of a quick temper.

"Oh, you mean the Sterlings?"

"Yeah." His voice was lower and more gravelly.

"You know them?"

"We've crossed paths a few times."

"Do you know Rashelle Harper? She works at the inn. She's a friend of mine, and I haven't been able to reach her since I got here last night."

"Sorry, the name doesn't sound familiar."

Disappointed he didn't know Shelle, Elizabeth grew more anxious about her friend's whereabouts and wondered if the guests should be concerned for their safety. Since he wasn't being more forthcoming, she couldn't resist testing the waters. "There seems to be somewhat of a cloud hanging over the Livingston mansion."

Ben, who had returned to drying the glasses, kept silent at that poke and averted his eyes.

She persisted. "I just learned that Lucretia Livingston lost her parents in a carbon monoxide poisoning not too long ago. How tragic."

The silent bartender cocked his head as if he suddenly developed a crick in his neck. "Yeah," he mumbled something imperceptible.

"Do you know Lucretia?"

"We have a . . . connection."

"And supposedly their deaths were ruled an accident, but there are those in town who question the role of their groundskeeper. Apparently he arrived on the scene not long before the poisonings. So maybe their deaths weren't accidental."

With raised eyebrows, he spoke softly, seeming to guard his reaction. "Hadn't heard. . . . Where did you hear that? It's news to me. People think their handyman—the gardener, whatever he was—they think he did it?"

"Certain people, yeah."

"Is that so?" He regarded her with a squint.

"What do you think?"

"Oh, what do I know," he snapped. "And what do people know. We're all just guessing . . . and wasting time doing it." The bartender grew quiet, unwilling to divulge much, so she pushed further.

"And what about Sterling? Do you know anything about him?"

"I know enough about him. And I hear things. Being a bartender you tend to hear about stuff more quickly than most other people in town, especially when your customers have had a few. They tend to get loose-lipped." His smirk took on a strange, almost sinister twist. Shifting his body away from her, he turned his attention to two jovial men who strolled through the open doorway, engaged in lively conversation until one noticed a patron at the far end of the bar.

"Mack! Was hopin' I'd find you in here." His voice bellowed above the chatter. More than a few people turned their heads at the disruption.

A man in a blue uniform with his sizable body hunched over a cup of coffee sat up straighter as the men approached. He acknowledged them with a nod and their first names. "Jeb . . . Dean."

Jeb seemed to be the gregarious one. Dean stayed silent.

"Thought you might want to know. I heard the *Selma Ann* broke loose from its mooring again."

The officer considered the news, nodding his head, clearly not alarmed. "That's it? You heard from someone? You don't know for sure, but someone mentioned it? In passing?"

"Thought you would want to check it out. It's happened before and—"

"Maybe this time the old geezer came back for his boat. Found a way to take it with him after all." Mack's chuckle had a sarcastic ring to it.

Wood scraped against wood as he stood, pushing his stool back, removing his wide girth from the counter and throwing his napkin onto the bar like a yellow flag on a football field. "Aw hell! Can't enjoy a goddamn cup of coffee without getting interrupted with this nonsense." Snatching the peaked cap from the counter, he jammed it down onto his head and stormed out.

Elizabeth noticed the shoulder patch on his way by. Boothbay Harbor Police Department.

Jeb and Dean took his place at the bar, pushing aside the coffee mug. Dean pulled the small plate with a half-eaten slice of cherry pie closer to him and picked up the fork to finish it off.

At that moment, the waitress sidled up next to Elizabeth with a tray filled from cleaning off a table. Glancing at a pad of paper with several lines scribbled on it, she transferred the dirty glasses to the bar without looking at them.

"Ben, I'm going to need a mimosa and another—"

"I gotta go." Before she could protest, he dashed for the door, grabbing a cowboy hat off the coatrack.

"Ben, the keys," she yelled, closing the distance between them.

Retrieving a wad from his pocket, he tossed them in a high arc and she snatched them out of the air.

"I'll be back," he called and slipped out.

Ana, as her name tag read, stood at the end of the bar glaring in Ben's direction, a dirty champagne glass clutched in one hand, the ring of keys dangling from an extended finger on the other.

"Damn it, Ben, I can't do your job *and* mine!" She threw the keys against the far wall, and they slid along the counter, coming to rest against a bottle of Jack Daniels.

Movement along the side windows caught the attention of the patrons seated in the booths as the bartender zipped past on the lavender bike.

"That son of a bitch. I *hate* when he does that. I don't know how he keeps his job. . . .Yeah, I do. I cover for him. Well, I'm done with that. He can explain for himself."

Unable to resist asking, Elizabeth ventured, "What's the *Selma Ann?*"

Ana groaned. "It's an old boat, probably a seventy-five footer, that was abandoned in the harbor after its owner passed away a year or so ago. Evidently he'd paid his mooring fees several years in advance, so no one has had a reason to boot it out of there. The guy that owned it was known for his big heart. If someone was down on his luck, he would try to help. Inviting homeless to stay on the boat until they could get back on their feet.

"Very generous."

"Yeah." She glanced back toward the doorway as if hoping Ben would appear again. "Well, these drinks aren't going to make themselves," she lamented, rounding the end of the counter to take on the role of bartender. Glass clinked as she tossed dead soldiers into the sink filled with cloudy water. And in true bartender fashion, she began to engage her closest patron as she pulled out clean glasses to fill. "So are you here just for the weekend?"

Returning a smile, Elizabeth offered, "Yeah, I've got a wedding to go to this afternoon."

Tipping a beer stein under the tap, Ana stayed focused on her work. "Nice. Where is it?"

Stunned to hear the inn had reopened, she dispensed with her task. Her eyes widened as she leaned in close and whispered, "I could use your help."

"*My* help?"

"Yes." Ana reached over and grabbed onto her wrist. "My best friend is missing . . . missing from the inn. She's married to Jonathon Sterling—oh I don't like that man. Never have. I'm afraid something terrible has happened to her."

"So how do you expect me to help?"

"I would never be able to get in there to look around. He knows me. Hates me."

A call from across the pub spurred Ana to scoop up the tray of drinks, make a loop through the room, delivering to tables scattered throughout. Returning hurriedly, she tossed the empty tray onto the edge of the bar. The clunk and rattle from it hitting the floor, tumbling over and over, failed to distract her.

"You can be my eyes and ears. We need to find out what's going on."

We? Suddenly Elizabeth felt herself getting pulled into a precarious situation. Then again, she was looking for her friend, too. *Was there a connection?*

"Why do you think she's missing?"

"Are you kidding? Lucretia and I are like sisters. Grew up here in town. Went off to college together. I know her parents weren't real keen on her venturing off so far—"

"Where'd you guys go?"

"Oral Roberts University out in Oklahoma."

"Oh, that *is* quite a distance. I only got as far as NYU. Grew up in Pennington Point."

Ana acknowledged the town with a nod. "Pretty area. And now you're back for a wedding?"

"Yeah. A high school friend is marrying someone from around here."

"I see. Well, Lucretia was *my* high school friend. In fact, we went all the way through school together. We were inseparable. Still are. I know something has happened to her. It's not like her to suddenly stop communicating with me. We always text or talk throughout the day."

"Have you gone to the police?"

"Of course, and supposedly they stopped out to the mansion, but I bet Sterling had some sort of plausible explanation why she wasn't there. I guess if her husband isn't concerned, and there's no reason for the police to believe she's been the victim of foul play, there's not much they can do."

"How long has it been since you've heard from her?"

Ana pressed her eyes closed as if pained to divulge the truth. "It's been a few days."

"You've got to admit that's not a terribly long time."

Ana shot her a glare.

"At least from law enforcement's point of view." Elizabeth tried to provide an alternate perspective.

"Perhaps. But I know something's up. Normally we talk every day. Several times a day. We never go this long without connecting. Even if we fight, which we rarely do, we usually are talking again within hours."

"And what do you think has happened?"

"I don't know. I just know something's wrong. I have a terrible feeling."

CHAPTER NINE

Pedaling *furiously*, he cursed the bike under his breath. It wasn't what Ben had envisioned his mode of transportation to be when he trekked cross-country to make a life for himself on the coast of Maine. The seat squeaked when he sat down on it or rolled over the slightest bump and made his ass sore. The rear brake pad rubbed against the rim, making an annoying "phith, phith" in sync with the speed he pedaled. He figured it would wear out the pad over time if he never got around to adjusting it, but he was more concerned about the hand mechanism. On the steep hills down to the wharf, he had to squeeze harder than ever to get the bike to slow down and stop when he needed it to. He'd worry about the mechanical issues another time. He suddenly had more pressing matters.

He needed to get to the boat before someone else did. Hopefully it hadn't drifted too far, and he could reach it with the dinghy he kept stashed along the shore. As long as it remained secured where the old man had left it, no one dared to question its right to be there. It was as if he still captained the *Selma Ann* as he had for decades. Passersby regarded it with deference. If it wasn't there, it would cause a stir, a veritable ripple in the water. But as long as it remained tied up to its mooring ball just off McFarland Island, the calm in the water would be maintained.

At the section of the road where it curved off to the right, away from the water, Ben pulled up to the edge and looked across the harbor. There, where it should be, was the *Selma Ann* bobbing with the incoming tide. She must have secured the boat on her own. It wasn't surprising she'd been able to, given her upbringing. She'd grown up around the water. Could handle herself in any kind of boat.

Relieved the immediate problem was resolved, Ben returned his ire to what had bubbled up in the latest gossip.

He had worked at the Livingstons' long before Sterling showed up on the scene. The son of a bitch waltzed in and whisked a vulnerable, much younger, and somewhat naïve but beautiful Lucretia off her feet. Ben didn't trust him. And you'd be hard pressed to find anyone who did. There was something about him that didn't set right with the townsfolk. Maybe it was the way he couldn't look you in the eye. Maybe it was how he looked down his nose at everyone, especially with that stiff-ass British accent of his. Perhaps the rub for Lucretia was he was always away, traveling on business, leaving her alone to fend for herself. Ben bet most people didn't even know what Sterling looked like, but he did. And the icy glare he'd seen more than once.

Ben didn't like the talk lately. And he certainly didn't appreciate hearing it from someone who was just visiting for the weekend.

That girl from Connecticut was entirely too nosy. Asking questions. What did she suspect? What did she already know? Assuring himself there was nothing for her to find, he decided her weekend visit would be over before she could become an amateur sleuth.

She was an outsider of sorts—staying at the Livingstons' place. He was an insider, but no one knew it. He knew the place intimately, like how the lock on the back window in the carriage house was broken. So even if the doors were padlocked, he could still get in and out. Probably saw parts of the inn the elder Livingstons didn't know existed or at least had never set foot into. Of course, they were no longer around. And he needed to be careful he didn't get tied to their untimely deaths.

Sterling didn't belong there, either. He was an evil, self-serving man driven by greed. Ben wondered if there'd ever been a genuine attraction between him and Lucretia. Ben was angry at her for falling for him. If only he'd met her before Jonathon showed up. Their get-togethers were limited to when Sterling was traveling. Or if they dared to chance it when he was in town, they stole away to a remote location where no one would recognize them. He only wished he could protect her, keep her safe from him. If anything ever happened to sweet Lucretia, the Brit would get everything. Had that been his plan all along? And if he ever found out Ben's connection to Lucretia, Sterling would be gunning for him. Ben knew he needed to make the first move.

CHAPTER TEN

Elizabeth *watched as the* waitress skillfully gathered her lunch plates with the dexterity of someone who'd been handling the task for years. Very little clinking. Certain items tucked under arms, others slid neatly onto the tray. Her badge read "Jo." Whether she'd been a waitress at the inn since its inception or was a recent hire, clearly she'd waited tables before and knew how to handle the china. Not knowing where her loyalties lay, Elizabeth decided to find out.

Upon her return with coffee pot in hand, Jo sidled up to the edge of the table as if she had all afternoon to talk and offered a refill in her perky voice. It was past the usual lunch hour, even for a Saturday, so there wasn't much of a crowd to speak of.

"Sure, I'd love half a cup. . . . Jo, I'm wondering if you can tell me more about the inn. It's absolutely beautiful with its picturesque setting on the harbor. What a fabulous find. I've got to return when I can stay longer. I'm thinking a girls' weekend away or a week of solitude when I can't stand work any longer."

"Where ya from?"

"I'm living in Connecticut, but I grew up on Pennington Point . . . in the inn there."

"Oh, that's just down the coast, isn't it?"

"Yeah. Not far at all." Elizabeth needed to direct her back to her original inquiry. "So coming from an old inn, I certainly appreciate this one. Do you know when it was built? Or how long it's been an inn?"

"I'm so glad you're enjoying your stay here. I don't know exactly when it was built. I know it was the family's estate before it became an inn. I'm sorry, I honestly don't know a lot about it."

"Who are the owners? Are they around? Maybe I could talk to them."

The waitress' eyes twitched ever so slightly. "Mr. and Mrs. Livingston—uh, Sterling are the owners. Ms. Livingston grew up in the house. Now they run it as an inn together."

"And are they on the property? Hands-on owners?"

"Yes, of course. Well, at least Lucretia is." She shifted her stance uncomfortably and repositioned herself farther away on the edge of the table, still clutching the pot. "Mr. Sterling pops in and out. He's not much for the day-to-day operations. He's more of a behind the scenes guy. A numbers guy. Lucretia is more of a cheerleader and seems to show up right when we need her. Everyone who works here loves her."

"A numbers guy? Like he handles the books?"

Jo hesitated. "Yeah. He signs my check every other week. That's all I need to know."

"I would love to meet Mrs. Sterling. Is there a certain time she stops in that I could catch her?"

"Unfortunately it's hard to say. She's so spontaneous we never know when it will happen."

"When did you see her last?"

Jo took a step away. *Did it sound more like an interrogation than a casual question?*

"I just would love to meet her," Elizabeth pressed.

Chuckling, Jo recovered slightly and tilted her head as if to say, "Your guess is as good as mine." Finally she offered, "Hopefully you'll get the chance before you leave."

With the awkward silence that ensued as Jo topped off her cup, it appeared she wasn't going to share anything more than her diplomatic answers. Either she knew nothing of interest or she was admirably loyal to her boss. The waitress dropped the check next to the saucer and then headed off to tend to the couple of other patrons.

Scribbling a tip and her signature that no one could possibly read, Elizabeth headed out, leaving her business card in plain sight on the table. She had a wedding to get to.

CHAPTER ELEVEN

The *quaint garden* behind the inn had been transformed into a sea of white. Folding chairs were neatly laid out in rows with an aisle down the middle. Small bouquets of white roses hung from the ends of the first couple of rows, designating special seating for family. A painted wooden arbor woven with white tulle stood at the end to serve as the altar. Even Mother Nature was cooperating with the intimate late afternoon affair. The briny sea air was heavy, full of summer heat, but the harbor provided somewhat of a reprieve with movement off the water. Some guests used their programs to fan themselves. Others had rolled them up and were fiddling with them.

In deference to those who'd had the decency to RSVP, Elizabeth sat in the back row on the bride's side and watched the event unfold like an uninvited observer. As guests trickled in and filled up the seats, the excited murmuring swelled. Ladies' wide-brimmed hats fluttered in the gentle breeze. A small boy fidgeted restlessly with his feet dangling above the soft grass, looking like he was itching to hop off and run through it. A man dressed as her grandmother would have deemed too casual for the momentous occasion meandered toward the arbor with a small black book tucked under one arm, looking decidedly uncomfortable. Justice of the peace?

With time to kill, Elizabeth tried Rashelle's number again. This time it went right to voicemail. Disappointed they weren't connecting, she realized she would have to stay at the inn one more night.

As a three-piece string ensemble warmed up off to the side of the altar, anxious guests stole glances toward the back to catch a glimpse of the bride. It was contagious. Elizabeth caught herself joining in. It had been a while since she'd spoken to or seen Natalia. Probably the last high school reunion. At the time, she looked good. Seemed happy. Of course, everyone put on airs, looking their best. But Natalia appeared genuinely content. She'd lost a lot of weight. So much so, Elizabeth wouldn't have recognized her without her name tag.

As she took it all in from the back row, she tried to be sincerely pleased for her high school acquaintance, fending off a twinge of envy, yet surprised to have received an invitation to such a personal occasion. It had the makings for a memorable day, one that would be documented in an album cherished by the bride and groom for years to come, if all went as planned.

The justice of the peace began to look as fidgety as the child at the end of the third row. Weddings notoriously started after the appointed time, but the hour was well beyond fashionably late. Blissful guests turned concerned, checking their watches and glancing to the rear more frequently. There were no groomsmen staking out their places at the altar and no groom in sight.

Sensing movement behind her, she turned to watch the bartender from Chauncey's enter as a mildly interested observer and strut to a spot along the row of junipers that framed the rear of the garden, his hands clasped behind him. As the breeze picked up and played with his hair, he ran his fingers through it to try to tame it. When he caught her eye, a pleasant unexpected ripple fluttered through her abdomen. He nodded his recognition. Of the fifty or so in attendance, he seemed the least concerned that something might be amiss.

Before long, guests were treated to the opening strains of Pachelbel's Canon and many looked visibly relieved to see the mother of the bride being escorted down the aisle. A barely audible sigh went out from the small group as guests settled back in their seats. Things appeared to be back on track, although still no sign of the groom.

The program only indicated who the bride's mother would be escorted by. There was no mention of the groom's parents. So next up would be the attendants. A maid of honor and two bridesmaids were listed, and they were talking quietly at the open French doors, decked out in strapless tea-length dresses that gave Elizabeth a craving for orange sherbet. From time to time, there was a glimpse of white behind them. The music swelled, and the dearly beloved turned in unison in anticipation of the big moment.

Just as the first bridesmaid stepped onto the garden path, a uniformed officer brushed past her on his way down the aisle with determined strides. Elizabeth recognized him as the guy from

Chauncey's that got called away from his coffee to check on an untethered boat. Clearly not invited to the party, he was there on official business. Holding up his hand to silence the musicians, he stepped up to the altar to face the crowd.

"Good afternoon, everyone. For those who don't know me, I'm Police Chief John McKenzie." He hesitated, presumably bearing the weight of his next words. "I'm afraid this afternoon isn't going to go as you all expected." He waited while collective gasps died down. "It appears that the groom, Natalia's fiancé, is missing." Another round of exclamations and outbursts swelled and died down again, allowing him to continue. "As many of you know, Edward is an employee here at the inn. The last time he was seen was on his shift Wednesday evening. He had Thursday and Friday off so he did not return to work, but no one else outside the inn that we have been able to determine has seen him since then either. His roommate says Edward didn't return back to his apartment Wednesday evening. We need your help; if you know anything, or you've seen him in the last couple of days, please let us know. Anything you might think of could be very important, no matter how trivial you think it is. . . . I'm sorry to have to tell you this. I know you came here to witness and participate in the celebration of two young lives being united in holy matrimony. Let's see if we can find him quickly and turn this into a happy ending."

The stunned guests sat motionless as the chief took his leave from the altar, slipping quickly from the uncomfortable spotlight. A shriek came from inside the French doors, followed by mournful sobbing. Elizabeth glanced back at the bartender. He was no longer there.

CHAPTER TWELVE

Some of the wedding guests remained pinned to their seats, still rapt at the police chief's news. Others scrambled to their feet, conferring with those around them, looking eager to jump in and help with the search.

Elizabeth considered her options. Suddenly with more time on her hands than she'd planned, she felt compelled to get into the mix and see what she could learn. Maybe she could help Ana find out about Lucretia's disappearance after all. Clearly something sinister had happened at the inn. Were the guests in danger? And where was her friend Rashelle? Were the three disappearances connected? She needed to do some digging. And the best place to start would be with the person who knew more about what went on than anyone else—the housekeeper.

Slipping away from the crowd, which was quickly becoming agitated, Elizabeth set off in search of the nearest cleaning lady. She didn't have to go far. As she approached the doors where the bride and her entourage had waited, she spotted a lady in a maid's uniform exiting the far set of doors. She took off down the walkway and darted around the corner with Elizabeth in pursuit.

"Excuse me!" Lizzi called but the woman didn't appear to hear her. She was off the clock and heading home, practically sprinting to her car. "Excuse me, ma'am?" Catching up to her on the sidewalk, Elizabeth reached out and gently took hold of the maid's upper arm. It slipped out of her grasp when the woman turned, yanking her arm away.

"Don't touch me," she snapped. The small plastic name tag pinned to her crisp gray and white standard-issue dress read, "Juanita."

Elizabeth took a step back, putting up an apologetic hand. "I didn't mean to offend. I just need to speak to you for a quick sec."

Juanita softened a bit. "I'm sorry, I don't have time." She spoke with a heavy Latino accent.

"Look, I know you just got off work and are anxious to get out of here, and you deserve to be able to do that. I know you work hard. I only need a minute of your time to talk to you."

"What about?"

Taking a step closer, Elizabeth lowered her voice. "I need to ask you if you've seen Mrs. Sterling recently."

The housekeeper's eyes flared, and she mumbled something that sounded like Spanish. "No, no! I haven't seen her. I have to go now." She turned away and started off toward her car again.

"Juanita, it's important," Elizabeth pleaded, catching up to her and staying on her heels. "Her best friend hasn't been able to reach her. She thinks she's missing. Do you have any reason to believe she might be?"

"I don't know anything about that," she called behind her as she rushed along. "I heard she was away for a few days . . . visiting family or a friend. Something like that."

"Do you know anyone who would want to hurt her?"

Her words made Juanita jolt to a stop.

"Could she be hurt? Is it possible she might need medical attention?" Elizabeth pressed.

"Lady, I don't know anything about such things."

"Who are you afraid of? If you know *anything* about it, you *have* to go to the police."

"No, no." She thrashed her head from side to side. "I can't. I don't know anything. There's nothing to know. Nothing to tell."

"She would want you to," Elizabeth threw out, hoping to appeal to her soft side, if there was any connection between her and Lucretia.

"I have to go." With that, she bolted toward an older model, sun-faded blue, foreign sedan with a dented front quarter panel. The driver's side was painted a matte yellow. Evidently the repairs were a work-in-progress. She attempted to start the stubborn engine a couple times before it actually turned over. Zipping in reverse out of the space, the clunker lurched forward, coughing and sputtering, leaving behind a dissipating cloud of blue smoke.

Striding back toward the main house, Elizabeth stopped at the stone wall along the side of the building, finding a shady spot to land on. Her eyes went to the open doors of the carriage house. A narrow tire stuck out from the bushes on the side. The fenders were lavender.

CHAPTER THIRTEEN

The paint on the stashed bike was faded. Familiar dents peeked through the foliage. As Elizabeth stepped into the open doorway, movement across the way caught her eye. Feet climbing the ladder disappeared into the loft that hovered over the far corner of the carriage house. The bartender's? What was he doing there? Did she dare confront him? With only a ladder to access the loft, she'd have to wait until he came back down. It would be foolish to follow him.

Retreating back out through the large opening, the breeze off the water caught her hair. A whirring out on the harbor grew louder, announcing the arrival of a seaplane taxiing up to the dock. Elizabeth didn't recall any local companies who flew regular routes into the Boothbay Region and wondered who was making such a grand entrance.

Two young men in dark green polos excused themselves as they brushed past her, jogging toward the dock. She watched as a tall, dark-haired man exited the plane with a briefcase in hand, directing the inn's employees to a small bag at his feet. He walked gingerly on the planks as if he was trying to get his land legs back. Once he hit dry land, he strode toward the inn with a confident gait, looking polished in his charcoal gray suit and crisp white button-down shirt. She imagined shiny gold cufflinks at each wrist and a neatly folded square tucked into his pocket. As he approached, his cell sprung to life with a jarring old-fashioned telephone ring, and he answered in a low, firm, slightly gravelly voice resonating with a delightfully British accent. His facial features were strikingly angular, as if he'd been carved from stone. Deep crevices accentuated the edges of his eyes cutting into his ghostly white skin and evidenced years beyond Elizabeth's.

Curious who the new arrival was, Elizabeth followed at a safe distance and entered the lobby after him. Owen at the bellman's stand greeted him with a hearty, "Welcome back, Mr. Sterling."

"Afternoon."

Elizabeth wondered if he knew his employees' names.

A startled young woman setting up afternoon tea in a corner of the lobby bobbled her tray, nearly sending it toppling to the floor. "Afternoon, Mr. Sterling," she managed, sidestepping to maintain her balance. He didn't acknowledge her greeting. A housekeeper near the top of the stairs whirled around wide-eyed at the sound of his voice and then scampered up the rest of the stairs. Elizabeth recognized Chip behind the reservation desk who offered a feeble, "Hello, sir" to his boss. Sterling shook his hand and engaged him in quiet conversation, and all the while Chip said very little, just nodding or shaking his head.

Detouring into the alcove provided for business travelers, Elizabeth settled in behind the desktop computer at the far end of the room and began searching for news stories about the Livingstons' tragic deaths. The local paper ran articles for a few days but seemed to limit their coverage out of respect for the victims. A more extensive article in the *Portland Herald* included quotes from interviews and photos of the victims and their estate. One picture that caught her eye was taken at the scene. It showed a crowd of people lined up behind yellow police tape, watching as men from the state medical examiner's office removed the cloaked bodies from the house on gurneys. Elizabeth enlarged the photo and scanned the crowd. Lunging toward the monitor to take a closer look, she recognized the unmistakable image of Ben the bartender in the front row.

The squawk of a police radio announced the arrival of Chief McKenzie, striding through the lobby, arms swinging at his sides as if he needed help to propel his excess weight. He made a beeline toward the front desk.

Elizabeth abandoned the computer to scoot closer to the action.

"Sterling," the chief called to catch him before he disappeared into the office behind the registration desk.

The innkeeper stopped short of entering but kept his back to the constable.

"I need to speak with you, sir." Rather formal for a small town.

"Certainly." He regarded his visitor. "I've just flown in, but I'd be happy to sit and have a chat with you, Mack. Always good to see you. We could grab a drink in the bar if you'd like. I'm sure I can scare up a bottle of Crown Royal—"

"It's not a social call, Jonathon." He kept to the serious business at hand.

Holding his gaze steady, Sterling complied. "Right then. Let's step into my office." He gestured toward the open doorway. As Mack passed through, Sterling asked Chip to let Lucretia know he'd arrived.

"Uh . . . uh, sir. We, uh, we don't know where she is. We haven't seen her in a couple days."

Sterling's face turned rigid. "What do mean? Have you tried her cell?"

"Yes, sir."

"Well, that doesn't make any sense. She knew I was returning." As if in an afterthought he added, "We had plans for dinner this evening." He sounded like a child, disappointed by a parent for having to cancel plans after an unexpected adult priority cropped up. "Did you try her friend, Ana?"

Chip nodded.

"Huh. All right, I'll see what I can find out after my meeting. . . . Anything else I should know about?"

"Uh . . . housekeeping is missing a laundry cart."

"Very funny."

"No, really, sir."

"Okay, well, let me know if anything serious pops up."

Once the two were securely behind the closed door, Elizabeth bolted over to the rack of brochures on the wall behind the front desk aimed at keeping out-of-town guests entertained. She feigned interest in a boat tour of lighthouses, a walking ghost tour, the Desert of Maine, hiking in Acadia, and an impressive array of outlets a short drive away, all the while listening to the muffled private conversation.

"You missed the nuptials."

"Yes, that was unfortunate. My business took longer than expected."

The chief brought Sterling up to speed on the wedding that never took place, acknowledging the absentee innkeeper probably wouldn't be able to shed much light on the situation. He asked about the intended groom and received standard stats as to his length of employment and position at the inn in return.

"It's certainly unsettling to hear the news. I don't know him well. Lucretia would be able to give you more background on him. She hired him when the mansion was first converted to an inn."

"Would you say they're close?"

Sterling let the question hang in the awkwardness of the implication. "Close? Well, as close as an employer and employee could be after working together for a couple of years. Lucretia is a tremendous boss. A real people person. She loves the staff. Ask anyone who works here."

"That doesn't surprise me one bit."

"Everyone loves her. If you ask me, I think she can be too much of a softie at times, but it seems to work for her."

"So am I to understand no one at the inn knows of her whereabouts at the moment?"

"Oh, I'm sure it's nothing to be alarmed about. With me away, I'm sure she comes and goes as she pleases. The staff are experienced and can handle the day-to-day operations. The inn hums along like a well-oiled machine now."

"That's not the impression I got from some of your employees. They said they're struggling to manage with a skeleton crew. Some are filling in positions they haven't been trained for. Apparently, while the inn was shut down for renovations, some people left and found work elsewhere and didn't return for the reopening."

"Yeah, things took a lot longer than they said it would. Apparently that's quite normal in this country. Such a dismal display of incompetence wouldn't be tolerated in England."

Ignoring his indignant tone, the chief continued. "Whose idea was it to renovate? It didn't look like it needed any work. It hadn't been operating as an inn for very long. What, two or three years?"

"Ahhh, but in this business you have to stay ahead of the game. There's a lot of competition out there. Look out the front windows. Everywhere you look there are inns and hotels in this town. You can't let things get so dated that guests start noticing. They'll go elsewhere. You need to be proactive."

"So it wasn't Mrs. Sterling's idea, was it? It was yours."

"Well, you can't fault me for being a shrewd businessman who's not afraid to invest in his holdings and knows when it's necessary."

"*Your* holdings? This was Miss Livingston's place *long* before you showed up."

Chuckling at the constable's not-so-subtle show of allegiance to the sweet hometown girl, he remained unprovoked. "That is true. However, now that we're working together on this venture, I think we make a great team. We balance each other. I've got astute business sense and can be tough when necessary. She's got the warm, fuzzy touch and handles personnel issues and guest relations quite naturally. I don't have the patience for that. But that's okay. I don't need to. That's her bailiwick."

"Surely Mrs. Sterling was upset when some of her key people didn't return. That must have created a gaping hole to lose experienced staff like that. But you can't blame them for seeking work elsewhere. You said yourself that the work took longer than expected. People need to earn a living for themselves, for their families."

"Of course, but that's all part of doing business. You're only as strong as your current staff. You can't be frittering away time worrying about the ones who didn't have enough sense to return. It's their loss. Not ours. You have to move on in these situations. Besides, we'd had an ongoing problem with pilfering. We've found silverware missing. Small paintings. And they were priceless ones that were in Lucretia's family holdings. If I were to guess, I would say it was the employees who didn't return who were responsible."

"Really. Would Mrs. Sterling agree with you on that?"

"Probably not. She doesn't have a sense for this kind of thing like I do. She's more hung up on who didn't return and why."

"So she *was* upset. Did you two have words about it?"

"Oh, come on, Mack. Let it go. You're making more out of this than need be."

"Perhaps. But she's unavailable to provide her side of the story."

"There are no sides here. Don't try to stir things up and start trouble—"

"I don't think I'm the one who has stirred things up."

Once an extended silence occupied the space beyond the door, Elizabeth scurried away, not wanting to come face-to-face with

Sterling after his encounter with the chief. Snatching a cup of Earl Grey and a couple shortbread cookies from the afternoon tea table, she slipped back into the drawing room where she could continue to observe the carryings-on yet remain out of sight.

Before long, Mack reappeared, crossing the lobby, scurrying out the way he came in.

CHAPTER FOURTEEN

A couple dripping water glasses in hand, Ana slid into the booth across from Elizabeth, plopping them down with a clunk. Buddy stirred at her feet but settled back down again. "So what have you found out?"

"Sterling got back today. Late this afternoon."

"Where's he been?"

"Don't know exactly, but apparently it had been quite a while."

"Yeah, I know where he's been. He's got an antiques business and goes abroad on buying trips. Stays away for long periods of time, leaving Lucretia to run the inn by herself. She hates it when he does that, but then she hates it when he returns and takes over. And he'll just show up unannounced."

Elizabeth considered the modest amount of luggage he'd gotten off the seaplane with for someone who'd been traveling for so long. But she would have to concede most guys traveled much lighter than she did. It was important to her to be prepared, have options.

"The police chief paid him a visit right after he got there."

"Really." The waitress scooted toward the edge of the bench.

"Yeah, he was looking for what Sterling knew about the missing groom."

Ana searched her eyes.

"The wedding I was supposed to go to this afternoon never got off the ground because the groom didn't show up. Interestingly enough, he's also an employee at the inn. Of course, Sterling couldn't tell him much. . . . I don't think he knows his employees."

"What's his name?"

"Edward something. I'd have to check my invitation. It's in my luggage at the room."

"Did they say anything about Lucretia?"

"The desk clerk mentioned the staff hadn't seen her in a couple days, but Sterling didn't seem all that concerned about it."

"Figures." Her eyes went to a steady stream of people walking past the window, like fish swimming in the same direction. One of the larger tour boats must have returned from a sunset sail. "I wonder if there's a connection between the two disappearances." She spoke as if to herself.

"I wonder the same thing." Elizabeth had already added a third name to the list.

Ana's focus returned to the pub. "It's certainly possible. I wouldn't rule it out." Leaning to one side, she retrieved something wrinkled and white from her back pocket. It looked like a legal-sized envelope folded in half. Elizabeth couldn't make out the handwritten block letters across the front as Ana unfolded it.

Her voice fell to a whisper. "Not too long ago, Lucretia gave this to me." She held it out for Elizabeth to see.

DO NOT OPEN UNLESS SOMETHING HAPPENS TO ME

The edge of the flap was jagged where it had been torn open, and the ink was smudged on a couple letters.

"So, what does it say?"

"Here, see for yourself." She shoved it in Elizabeth's face.

"That's okay. Seems kinda personal." She sat back against the seat, throwing a dismissive hand up. If it was possible to pull prints from paper, she didn't need to add hers.

"It *was*. Now it's evidence. I opened it this morning. I *knew* something was wrong." She shook it at her. "She says right in here if anything happens to her, the first person they should question is Sterling." Slipping out and unfolding a single sheet of paper, she read Lucretia's words:

> *If something happens to me, look no farther than Jonathon Sterling. In the short time we've been married, I've been the victim of numerous physical outbursts, suffering bruises and contusions at his hands which I've endeavored to hide from everyone around me. I fear if anyone grew suspicious and confronted him, Jonathon*

*would turn his temper on me and retaliate.
There's a fury within him we have only
seen a glimpse of. And while that doesn't
sound like anything to act on, I've seen
it in his eyes. I live in terror. Something's
brewing from his past that he is intent on
avenging. God help anyone near him when
he does.*

Lucretia Livingston Sterling

"The poor thing." Elizabeth loathed the man.

"God, I hope she's all right. What a terrible friend. I never caught on, and she was afraid to tell me."

"Don't be so hard on yourself. Sounds like she worked hard to keep it from everyone. The police chief should take a look at that."

"Absolutely. Usually he comes in here for dinner. I was going to give it to him then, but he didn't stop in tonight."

"I imagine he's got his hands full."

"Yeah, I'll have to track him down." She refolded the note, slipped it back into the envelope, and returned it to the pocket it came from.

"Let me ask you about my friend, Rashelle Harper, who works at the inn. I haven't been able to contact her since I arrived, and I'm getting worried about her, too. Do you know her? I call her Shelle, but I guess they refer to her as Shelly."

"The name isn't familiar. Has she been there long?"

"No, she was a recent hire."

"Oh, that's probably why I haven't heard Lucretia mention the name. My God, we're dealing with three disappearances from the inn. What the hell is going on?"

Leaving Ana's open-ended question alone, Elizabeth continued. "I also want to ask you about the bartender I met this morning."

"Ben?"

"Yeah. What's his story?"

"Don't know all that much about him. He and I never really clicked. Everyone else seems to like him. Has a lot of regulars that stop in to have a drink or two and chat with him. I don't trust him, though. Don't know what his deal is. Plays it very close to the chest. Sometimes it feels like he's watching me, keeping an eye on me. I'm sure I sound paranoid."

"Not necessarily." She didn't know her or her situation well enough to make that call.

"And he's got this annoying habit of taking off in the middle of his shift. Like he did earlier. I'll see him on his cell, and then he disappears. Drives me nuts. And I have to cover for him. No one cares about it but me."

"Do you know where he lives?"

"That's hard to say. I get the impression he doesn't stay in one place very long."

"How long has he worked here?"

"Why all the questions? Do you think he's involved somehow?"

"I don't have any specific thoughts. Just thinking of possibilities. So . . . how long has it been?"

"He started a few months before I did."

"Which was . . . ?"

She threw her back against the booth's veneer. "Jeez, it's been over three years already. Hard to believe." Her jaw tightened as she leaned in. "Ya know, I was not planning to come back here after I graduated. I'd had my fill of this small town. It's such a dead end. I wanted to get out. Start somewhere new. But here I am. Still working in a nowhere job that was supposed to be only until I could get my first real job out of college."

"So why'd you come back? . . . For Lucretia?"

Ana's eyes followed a car passing by the window. "Yeah, I had to. What kind of friend would I have been if I hadn't? I was the one who convinced her to go all the way out west for college. Her parents didn't want her to go, but she finally talked them into it. Then they died, and she was so far away. . . . She dropped out to come back. Never finished. I felt so bad for her."

"No one could have known—"

"I know, but it doesn't help me feel any less guilty. For the longest time I didn't hear from her after she left school. Didn't respond to texts. Didn't return my calls."

"Did she ever say why?"

"Not really. And I didn't press. I don't think it was just me. She cut herself off from the rest of the world, too. I think it was part of her mourning process."

"How did she meet Sterling?"

"Something to do with his antiques business. I think she may have been selling off some pieces. They met while I was still away at school so I wasn't around to steer her clear of him. It couldn't have been long after her parents died."

"You would have warned her off?"

"Absolutely. How could she be thinking straight under the circumstances? And how can you possibly get to know someone in such a short time? Somehow the son of a bitch wooed her, and they married pretty quickly. He had no right to play on her vulnerability. Once I graduated and dragged my sorry ass back here, we reconnected. I was shocked when I heard the news."

"I understand he's from England? Is that where his business is based?"

"No. His family has their own antiques business there. He has older brothers that took over for their father, but they never let Sterling get involved. He came over here to start off on his own, make a name for himself. From what I understand he's never forgiven his brothers for keeping him out of it. And he's determined to do whatever it takes to be successful and prove he could do it without them."

"Sounds a bit pathetic."

"Yeah, I figure something had to have happened. I mean who treats family like that?"

"So now, back to Ben. You said he's worked here for over three years. He started before you came back. Would that make it around the time of Lucretia's parents' deaths?"

Ana fell silent.

"Yeah."

Elizabeth scooted toward her. "Ana, I did some digging online this afternoon. I found something rather interesting." She slipped her cell out of her pocket and pulled up the article with the photo of Ben in the crowd. Handing over her phone, she asked, "Does he have some sort of connection with the Livingstons?"

"Hard to say." She squinted at the photo until her eyes grew wide. "Could be he was an innocent onlooker like everyone else."

Elizabeth wasn't as quick to justify his presence at a crime scene as mere curiosity.

The buzz of conversation in the pub dropped off as if a volume knob had been turned down.

Ana popped up, bumping the edge of the table. "Uh oh."

"What?"

"The bell." Sliding out of the booth, she darted across the pub.

"The what?" Elizabeth called after her, and then she could hear it. A church bell clanged somewhere in the distance. Ana disappeared through the open doorway, and the rest of the pub cleared out behind her, creating an eerie silence with the bell tolling in the background.

What did it mean? Where was everyone going? Lizzi had every intention of finding out. "Come on, Bud."

Despite their efforts to catch up with Ana, she was swallowed by a swarm of townsfolk that burgeoned into an impressive crowd by the time it reached the stately white church up the hill overlooking the harbor, awash in spotlights at the foot of the structure. Streetlights cast shadows of the mature trees dotting the property. The bell clanged incessantly, raw metal against metal, inciting an urgency Elizabeth failed to comprehend. Only intending to be an observer, she hung back on the lawn while others pressed close to the dusty red brick steps that led up to double wooden doors painted black. Her pup sat close at her feet with a front paw pressed on the top of her foot.

Soon they were surrounded by others responding to the clanging. Anxious murmurings swelled as they checked in with each other, eager to know why they'd been summoned. Heads shook and faces twisted into grimaces of concern. Soon the size of the mass behind her matched that of the earlier arrivals. The crowd's movement was fluid as curious onlookers jostled for position, condensing the space between their bodies. Elizabeth fought off the unsettling sensation of feeling trapped. A sharp elbow to her side took her breath away. Buddy leaned hard against her leg. The bell clanged on. She pulled in air in short gasps, holding tight to his collar.

As the bell fell silent, a hush moved through the crowd. All movement ceased. It was as though they knew what was coming next. Before long, one of the doors opened and Chief McKenzie appeared, stepping out onto the top step into the glare of an overhead light, like an actor on a stage. He surveyed those assembled in front of him.

"You know what I'm about to say isn't going to be good." The townsfolk remained still. A few heads nodded. "Thankfully, it's been a while since we've had to ring the bell. But tonight we have a young man to find."

The chief laid out the details of the wedding gone wrong and where young Edward was last seen, imploring everyone to join in the search and to report any information that could assist the authorities. After the swell of concerned outbursts subsided, he made his way down the steps. Ana emerged from the front of the pack and lunged at him, grabbing him by the elbow, no doubt lamenting about her dear friend, Lucretia.

As the crowd dispersed, Elizabeth felt a tug on her arm. It was Florence from the historical society. She didn't recognize her at first, clothed in twenty-first century attire.

"Florence, do you know the guy from the inn the police chief was referring to? Sounds like something awful has happened for him to miss his own wedding."

"I know who the family is . . . but I don't really know him." Brushing off her question, she continued. "See that guy over there?" She nodded toward the silhouette of a man leaning up against a broad oak, arms folded across his chest. Stepping closer, she spoke into Elizabeth's ear, lightly grazing her cheek. "He was the Livingstons' groundskeeper at the time of their deaths. I haven't seen him in quite a while, but I wouldn't forget a good lookin' guy like that."

"Are you sure? He's a bartender at Chauncey's."

"Well, I don't make a habit of frequenting bars, so I wouldn't know where he's employed now."

"How do you know he was there then?"

"As I mentioned, Miranda Livingston, Lucretia's mother, was a dear friend. . . . I know a lot about what went on at the Livingston estate over the years."

"And you think he had something to do with their deaths?" Elizabeth reminded herself that the photo of Ben in the front row of the crowd observing the medical team removing the bodies was not evidence of guilt, but she found it hard to separate the two. Too many fingers pointed in his direction.

"I don't know. . . . There's something about him that bothers me. Not only me. I'm not alone in this."

"What would his motive be?" Elizabeth pressed. "He happened to roll into town and somehow talked them into hiring him as their handyman? You don't think it was a coincidence that he ended up there?"

"*Nothing* is a coincidence." In the dim light of a nearby lamppost, the old woman's eyes grew stern.

"Do you think there's a connection between the bartender and what's going on now at the inn?"

"Absolutely. No question in my mind. I don't know what he's up to, but I would keep an eye on that one."

"Is there bad blood between him and Sterling?"

"Could be. You'd have a hard time finding anyone in this town who would take Sterling's side. No one likes him. No one *trusts* him."

"So we're talking about two men who people don't trust. Any chance they could be in cahoots with one another?'

"Ooh, that's entirely possible."

"Doing what?"

Florence fell silent. Apparently she hadn't thought through all of her allegations.

Upon her return to the inn, the beat-up lavender bike was no longer stashed in the bushes alongside the carriage house, but the doors facing the water were still open as if inviting her to step inside. An overhead lantern cast a dim light into the space, making the shadows beyond look as dark as the night sky with a new moon. Switching on her cell's flashlight, she stepped in, passing an old horse-drawn carriage and an even older sleigh. The ladder to the loft beckoned. Grabbing a rung at eye level, she pulled herself up, hand over hand.

At the top, she found what looked like a long-forgotten and cluttered storage area. No obvious sign of Ben amidst the mess. She hauled herself up over the top rung and scrambled onto a dusty, dark-stained wooden floor that gave way slightly, creaking under her feet. Fearing she had revealed her arrival, she scanned between the furnishings as she crept.

Windsor chairs stacked haphazardly on top of one another to the left looked like they could come toppling down with the slight movement of someone brushing past. Paint-dripped cans from projects long since finished formed a wall just past them. Larger pieces of furniture Elizabeth tried to imagine being hauled up the ladder filled in the rest of the space and were pushed tightly together, their sheer weight looking like they would take down the entire loft with the next sneeze. Beyond a stack of square moving boxes, with the name of a company she wasn't familiar with, were folded vinyl tarps piled waist high on the far wall. She'd reached the end.

With the unmistakable feeling of eyes on her back, she froze.

Whirling around, she expected to be trapped by a man with broad shoulders and rippling muscles, whose motives she had yet to discern. Relieved it was only a barn owl perched on the railing whose saucer-like eyes sized her up, she doubled back across the loft, sending him swooping in the opposite direction. Her eyes went to a shipping blanket draped over an old rolltop desk. Lifting it, she knelt down to discover a bedroll underneath with an unzipped duffle next to it. An unlit tapered candle stuck out of a wine bottle with wax dripped in bumpy tracks down the sides. Leftover from a romantic tryst? If so, who with? Lucretia? He did say they had a connection.

A light flashed on the wall from below. Elizabeth reeled at a creaking rung, letting go of the corner of the blanket, and turned her phone against her abdomen to keep her presence concealed as long as she could. *Who was on their way up?* Someone from the staff doing their rounds? There was nowhere for her to retreat to. It was too late to scoot under the desk. She'd have to think of something to justify a guest nosing around a dark loft.

The bobbing light popped over the top rung. Elizabeth flashed hers in the same direction.

"Ben?"

He jolted still and shined his light on her. "Well, not who I would have expected to run into up here." Heaving himself up over the last rung, he sprung to his feet and strode toward her, encroaching on her personal space, glaring from his six-inch height advantage.

"What are you up to, Ben?"

"What makes you think I'm up to something?"

"Is that your stuff under the desk?" What was she opening herself up to? How much more vulnerable could she be than being twenty feet off a hard-packed dirt floor, and her only way out was through a rugged cowboy who could do with her what he wanted?

"What stuff?"

"You know what I mean. There's even a pair of cowboy boots. Your spare pair, I presume?"

"I'm sure they belong to someone else," he scoffed, swatting at the air.

"Well, then, what are you doing up here?" She was probably pushing her luck, but she had to at least try.

Averting his eyes, he mumbled, "I needed a place to stay for a while."

"You're living up here?" She glanced around the loft.

"I let a friend crash on my boat. . . . And it's not really big enough for the two of us, so I came here."

He followed her darting eyes and chuckled.

"You're sleeping under a desk?"

"Just for a couple days."

"Do you really think no one will figure it out? Like Sterling? I doubt he'd be too pleased to find a non-paying guest."

"I'm a hell of a lot smarter than he is, and I bet I know this place better than he does, too."

"How's that?"

Leaving her question unanswered, he lowered his beam to the floor. "You wouldn't want him to catch you up here."

Voices below sent them dropping to their hands and knees. As they listened, a police radio squawked on its way past the open doorway.

"You need to get out of here," he whispered with an unspoken, "before you blow it for me."

"What about you?"

"Just get out already. . . . And don't come back up here. I don't need anyone nosing around." He grabbed her wrist.

"*I* did. What's to stop—" He squeezed hard enough to cut off her circulation. "Ugh. Please . . ."

"Just go." He was through chatting.

CHAPTER FIFTEEN

Pacing the halls was accomplishing nothing other than wearing a path in the carpet. Sterling worried for Lucretia. His bride had slipped through his fingers. She was gone. How could he have been so careless? He'd been away too long.

Regrettably, weeks away turned into months because he'd had to keep looking until he found the right pieces. The perfect antiques to impress everyone. The buyers. But more importantly at the next auction, his brothers. They never would have expected little Jonathon to come up with such finds. . . . He expected that's how they still considered him. Little. Always the kid brother they could push around. Damn them for shutting him out of the family business their father worked so hard to build over the years. He would show them. They'd regret their selfishness and shortsightedness.

His restless spirit guided him past silent doors where guests slept soundly, probably never questioning their safety at the inn.

Slipping out into the still of the night onto the courtyard, an eerie mist illuminated by the moon hung in the air. He hoped the night chill would help to clear his head so he could sleep. A loop through the grounds would satisfy him nothing was amiss. He knew that included the old cemetery beyond the yard. It was the middle of the night. Was that where he wanted to be? He would make a quick pass-through.

Ascending the crumbling stone steps, his feet sunk in where the treads gave way to disrepair. A twinge of guilt reminded him Lucretia had begged him to spend money on restoring her ancestors' burial ground. He'd felt there were more pressing issues that needed addressing at the inn and took the heavy hand to ensure they were taken care of.

Reaching the top, he scanned the half-acre laid out before him. It looked worse in the moonlight than he remembered it appearing in the brilliant sunshine. He looked away so he didn't have to read the names that had yet to be obscured by overgrown grass.

Uncomfortable to be sharing the moonlight with his wife's dead family, Sterling took a step backward onto uneven ground. Shifted off balance by too many late-night brandies, he fumbled to regain his stance but failed to recover. He spun a quarter turn with flailing arms, landing face first onto a heap of fresh dirt in the corner against the stone wall.

"Bloody hell!" he swore under his breath, pulling himself to his feet, wiping off his front side. "This cemetery is a lost cause." No one was within earshot to argue the point.

Anxious to escape the wall encircling the generations of Livingstons, Sterling redirected his steps through the courtyard toward the carriage house. That would be worth a walk-through as well.

Reaching the broad wooden doors, he shoved one panel aside and stepped into the dark space, listening for a sound. Any sound. Nothing. He reached back and flipped the switch. The lone bulb hanging from the ceiling sprung to life but did little to illuminate the large space.

"Hello!" He thought it was worth trying. "Anyone here?" Just the chirping of crickets somewhere on the perimeter of the building. All seemed in order. Sliding the large wooden door closed, he jolted at the voice behind him.

"Kind of late, isn't it, Mr. Sterling?"

Turning into the glare of a flashlight beam, he squinted and put a hand up to shield his eyes.

The officer tilted his head, and the corner of his mouth turned up. "Wow. Looks like you've got quite a mess on your hands and then some." He chuckled, clearly pleased with himself. "Sir, what kind of a project you got goin' on that you have to handle it yourself?"

Jonathon's eyes ran down his soiled clothes, and he did his best to look indignant. "It takes a lot of hard work to run a place like this, and the work is never done. I bloody well get my hands dirty alongside the staff, Jenkins." He used the back of his soiled hand to wipe a brow intersected by a jagged childhood scar, evidence of a tumble down the stairs, courtesy of one of his older brothers.

The officer glanced at his watch. "Yes, sir, but at three o'clock in the morning?"

"Ahhh, time got away from me. You know how 'tis, you get along working on something, and you completely lose track of time." Irked by the constable's unannounced visit, Sterling was anxious to get rid of him.

"But what could possibly be so important that it couldn't wait until morning? You Brits have an odd work schedule." He shifted his light away from Sterling's face and onto the side of the carriage house, reflecting a soft glow on himself.

"Well, I did just get back from a trip abroad. Maybe I'm still on London time." He laughed, aghast that it had a nervous warble to it, but hoping to satisfy the cop's curiosity.

"Oh, why were you across the pond? Visiting family? Business trip?"

"Both, actually. I go abroad often, searching for pieces for my business. The depth of the antiques pool here pales in comparison to what's available there, and I always stop in to see my mum in Liverpool." He was growing impatient with the annoying questions. None of his damn business. *Keep an even face.*

"I see. But you still didn't tell me what was so important, it couldn't wait," Jenkins prodded.

Searching for an answer to appease him, Sterling maintained a steady expression and then calmly blurted out the first thing that came to mind. "If you must know, I've got plans to pour a concrete floor." He nodded toward the double doors. "I'm starting to clean out the place. It's amazing how much has accumulated over time."

"Concrete? Won't that take away from the integrity of the building? It *is* an old carriage house dating back to the turn of the century. Obviously they didn't use concrete back then."

Stunned the guy was so concerned about architectural integrity at that hour, Sterling held firm. "'Tis true, but from a practical standpoint, it makes more sense to have the concrete. Storing our modern-day equipment and housing the old carriages on a dirt floor has its drawbacks. The dampness in the ground doesn't do us any favors."

The officer's eyes softened as if he were becoming convinced of the project's validity, and Sterling was relieved to have come up with a viable out. He didn't like anyone, particularly a small-town cop, snooping around the property.

"There's a lot that has to be done first, which I can only fit into my schedule late at night. Besides, I want to surprise Lucretia when she gets back from her holiday visiting a friend."

"I see. So I can tell your nosy, insomniac neighbor that nothing out of the ordinary is going on. You're a night owl with a big project on your hands."

"I'd appreciate that."

"All right then. I'll be on my way. Say hello to the missus for me."

"Will do."

CHAPTER SIXTEEN

Tossing the camera on the front seat, Ben ran his hand under the floor mat, catching his fingers on the key just where he expected it to be. The bright red plastic lobster hanging from the ring seemed overly touristy for a local. His family wasn't even in the lobstering business. Tough to figure but not worth spending time on.

Jamming the key in the ignition, the old girl resisted on the first attempt as if she knew he wasn't her rightful owner. "It's okay. Edward said it was all right to borrow you when I needed to. And tonight, I need to. Come on, girl." A second try and she roared to life. He let the pickup run for a couple minutes before heading out. "Besides, I don't think he'll be coming by anytime soon."

Once he pulled up to his lookout spot, he switched off the lights. The engine's idle was rough, like it had been years since its last tune-up. Ed probably hadn't wanted to spend money on the truck, what with all the expenses of the wedding. Didn't look like he'd be needing it any more. Perhaps Ben would have to shell out a wad to keep it running so it would be there when he needed it. He didn't exactly have a lot of extra cash jangling in his pocket, just keys.

The vibration rocked Ben gently, nearly lulling him into a doze. He shut it off to save gas. No telling how long it would be before she showed her face. And she often went out the back as if she knew someone was keeping an eye on her. Relieved to have the cover of darkness, he felt fairly comfortable spending so long in the same location.

Movement caught his eye, and he followed a shadowy figure out from the back of the house up on the hill and into the open door of the freestanding double-bay garage. He watched as the rear lights of a vehicle turned on, then the back-up lights. As the car backed down the short driveway and pulled out into the street, Ben ducked, catching the silhouette of her father at the wheel before he sped off down the street.

He didn't have to wait long before another figure emerged from the house and slipped around to the back of the garage. His person of interest? Before long, the open garage door closed while the other opened. He ducked down again as the Volkswagen bug backed into the turnaround and drove nose first down the drive, headlights lighting up the inside of the cab.

He turned the key and the engine turned over with a groan. Before long, he had caught up to her—but not too close. She was heading to one of her usual spots. This time he had the camera for proof.

CHAPTER SEVENTEEN

Despite the early hour, he'd fished the whiskey bottle out of his desk drawer and filled his glass, still sticky from the night before, a healthy third of the way up the side. It was time to contact local law enforcement about his missing wife, and he needed to take the edge off.

Gulping the last swig, he picked up his cell and dialed. After two rings a female voice answered, asking where to direct his call.

"Yes, I'd like to speak to Chief McKenzie, please. It's Jonathon Sterling."

After a couple clicks that sounded like he'd been disconnected, a rough voice came on and Sterling began his well-rehearsed story, layering in his angst. The chief stopped him a few sentences in and told him he'd come right out. Probably had nothing else going on and needed something to keep himself occupied and looking like he was earning his salary.

Before long, Mack pulled up to the portico as if he were checking in. Sterling almost expected the lights on the cruiser to be flashing. Probably didn't get to turn those on very often.

After a handshake and an exchange of concerned looks, they set off for a stroll around the estate so as not to arouse the staff's curiosity.

"So when exactly did she go missing?"

"Apparently it was a couple nights ago—"

"And you waited until now to say something? You weren't concerned yesterday," the chief snapped.

"Well, I had just arrived when you showed up for a chat. And to be honest, once I realized she wasn't at the inn, I thought she'd stormed off and went to stay with a friend for a while."

"So you two had a fight?"

"No, we didn't have a fight. I think she may have gotten a bit hot and bothered when I didn't arrive back home when I originally said I would."

"What did you fight about?"

"Again, it was not a fight," he corrected calmly, motioning for the chief to lower his voice. "I texted her to let her know I'd be delayed a few more days. My travels kept me away longer than expected, and if she was upset, she deserved to be."

"So you know she was upset? Did someone on the staff tell you that? Edward perhaps?"

"No, I don't know for a fact that she was angry," he clarified. "I'm surmising it's entirely possible . . . probable. You can't tell someone's tone of voice from a text."

"You texted her? You didn't call to speak to her directly? Not very intimate for newlyweds—you are still newlyweds, aren't you?"

"Well, sure." He wasn't going to let an overpaid, overweight constable, whose salary was courtesy of taxpayers, twist the story to suit him. "We text often. Besides the matter of the time difference, we're both quite busy, so it's an efficient way of communicating that doesn't take too much time out of—"

"So you let her know you weren't showing up as planned, and you arrived Saturday afternoon right before we spoke in your office about Edward."

"That's correct."

"And she didn't know exactly when you were showing up?"

"No, I wanted to surprise her. And I had planned to make it all up to her with a nice dinner that evening."

"Did you try calling around to check with her friends . . . once you noticed she was missing?"

"No, she's a grown woman. She doesn't need her husband checking up on her, giving her friends the impression we'd had a fight. I figured she would calm down and come back when she was ready. She simply needed some space . . . and time."

"Do you guys fight often?"

"Again, it was not a fight—"

"Certainly sounds like one to me."

"Well, it wasn't," Sterling insisted, pulling back from the exchange. He had to be careful not to get drawn in by the chief's bait. "We texted back and forth a couple times and then that was it. As you mentioned, we've only been married a short time. Hardly long enough to have a reason to fight."

"So you finally decided it was serious enough to bring me into the picture." His tone dripped with annoyance.

"I kept thinking she was going to walk in the door any minute or at least text me to say where she was. Then it hit me that Wednesday was the last time anyone had seen her, certainly longer than would seem necessary to cool off if she was mad. Mack, I'm afraid something has happened to her. Please help me find her."

The chief cocked his head, as if assessing his sincerity. "We'll do everything we can. Mind if I take a look around?"

"Of course not. It's all yours," he offered with an open palm.

"I'm going to call in some backup as well."

"Absolutely. I'd appreciate that. And let me know how I can help." He shoved his hand deep in his pocket and fondled its contents.

"Would you mind if I have a look at your phone?"

"Not at all. Anything in particular?"

"Specifically at the texting conversation between you two. It would give me a better idea of the sequence of events . . . the time frame we're talking about."

"Oh, well, I'm afraid there's nothing for you to see. I was having trouble with my battery running down too quickly, so I deleted a bunch of stuff on my phone—including some useless text conversations that were taking up a dreadful amount of space."

"Isn't that a shame."

CHAPTER EIGHTEEN

After a restless night's sleep for both of them, Elizabeth left behind the musty room with its odd furnishings and busy wallpaper to head outside with her pup. As they descended the grand staircase, Sterling fidgeted behind the front desk as he carried on with someone on the other end of the phone.

"Yes, I understand that your boat is at the dock, waiting for someone to pick up our delivery. You've called three times to tell me that." His voice grew agitated. "We're a little understaffed right now—" His open-faced hand chopped at the air like a butcher on a side of beef. "Look, I didn't know we had ordered anything. Can you just leave it there for the time being? It's on ice, isn't it?" Covering the receiver with his palm, he bellowed toward the back office, "Chip, you back there?" When no answer came, he tried again, "Juanita, where are you?" No response.

As the duo reached the bottom of the stairs, Sterling looked up, lifting a brow at a dog in his lobby. His eyes darted to Elizabeth, and his face softened. "I'll get someone out there. Give me a minute." He slammed down the phone but didn't take his focus off of her.

What had looked like sculpted features from a distance took on the semblance of a drawn, aging complexion up close. His dark, penetrating eyes stood in striking contrast to his pale skin. A dark mole near his lips gave him a strange feminine quality like a fifties movie star.

"Well, good morning," he called in a sickeningly sweet, eager-to-please, slippery tone that exaggerated his British accent. "We haven't had a chance to meet yet. Jonathon Sterling, love." He extended his hand as he rounded the counter. It was cold, clammy, and limp. They shook, and a strange tingle ran up Elizabeth's arm. She yanked her hand away, desperately wanting to wipe it on her pants, but instead she settled for the soft warm fur on Buddy's broad side.

"Elizabeth Pennington," she offered with restrained enthusiasm. His overpowering aftershave made her nose wrinkle, but his expertly tailored suit and crisp white button-down almost made up for it.

"Pleased to meet you, Miss Pennington. What a pleasure. I hope you will be staying with us for a while. How are you finding the inn so far? Is everything to your liking?"

Sidestepping his gushing, she redirected him. "And this is Buddy."

"I see." He regarded the canine with disdain, which Elizabeth ignored. "You've brought a furry creature with you." Struggling to maintain a smile, he clearly disapproved. "What cottage are you staying in?"

"Uh, we're not. We're up on the second floor."

"The second floor . . . in a room." He blinked his eyes deliberately until he could get them under control.

"I'm sorry, dogs aren't allowed in the main inn?"

A sickening feeling crept into her stomach. The guy at check-in didn't act like it would be an issue. Clearly he wasn't expecting Sterling's arrival.

He paused for a moment, perhaps for effect. "Well, not entirely. Usually we put dog people in one of the cottages, but undoubtedly one wasn't available when you checked in because of the construction delays. The whole project ran ghastly over budget and over schedule." The last word he pronounced as if there was no "c."

Dog people? Really? Clearly *he* wasn't one.

Elizabeth stepped backward, putting some distance between them. She didn't think she was going to like him. And he was giving her no reason to allow him the benefit of the doubt.

"We'll let it slide this time. Lord knows there's nothing we can do about it now."

Elizabeth searched his eyes for a hint of sarcasm and found none.

"Oh, and if you need pooper scooper bags so you can clean up after your furry friend, we can supply them to you. We pride ourselves on the cleanliness of our beautiful grounds. We wouldn't want other guests to have the misfortune of sullying their soles because of a negligent guest."

She held her gaze steady.

"They're scented."

Really? This guy was not helping his cause. "We're all set. Thanks."

Moving on, she turned the focus away from her innocent pup.

"Sounds like you have a bit of a conundrum on your hands this morning." She couldn't resist poking at the self-absorbed stuffed shirt.

"Well, it will all be straightened out in due time. One of the staff will happen along that I can rope into doing the errand for me and—"

"Or you could just do it yourself."

His face fell almost unperceptively. "Well, I don't think *I* should have to—"

"I mean . . . I don't know that I would leave a crate of fresh fish at the end of a dock for anyone to pick up. Especially the seagulls."

He considered her suggestion. "You do make a valid point. Perhaps I should take care of matters straight away. After all, these guns should be able to handle it without a problem." He flexed his biceps like a bodybuilder on the beach, looking to Elizabeth for a reaction. He got none.

"Before you go, I wonder if I could trouble you for the address of my friend, Shelle—Shelly, your new day manager. I haven't been able to reach her since I arrived, and I was hoping to catch up with her before I leave."

"I'm sorry, Miss Pennington, I'm afraid I can't give out personal information on our employees. I'd be happy to have someone give her a call for you."

"Don't bother. I've tried that, and she doesn't answer. I'm just getting a little worried and was hoping to stop by her house."

"I'm sorry. I can't. She's off until Monday, but if she calls in before then, we could give her a message for you."

Frustrated with his inability to comprehend the seriousness of the situation and his unwillingness to help, she mumbled, "Never mind."

With no further words between them, he brushed past her to tackle his unpleasant task.

Elizabeth dialed Shelle's number again, and her call went straight to a message with a female voice declaring her mailbox was full.

Nestled toward the back of the inn and renowned for its award-winning seafood entrees, *Sea Salt* received daily deliveries of fresh fish and lobsters from local fishermen at the dock across the street. Unable to delegate the menial task, Sterling reluctantly headed down the circular drive toward the harbor dressed more appropriately for greeting guests at the registration counter than picking up a dripping box of smelly crustaceans. He'd have someone's head for this.

"Damn it! I don't know why the *bloody* hell no one seems to be around," he grumbled to himself.

Arriving at the long wooden dock, he was surprised to see the boat idling noisily at the end, tied up on its port side, bobbing in the water, pointing out toward open sea. He thought the boats usually came alongside and tied up closer to shore, but he didn't have a lot of experience to draw on. Someone was at the controls, but he couldn't see the captain's face very well. The figure wore a baseball cap and sunglasses. The captain waved yet didn't budge from the wheelhouse. With Sterling's first step onto the dock, his feet froze before he could move any farther. Suddenly, the dock grew narrower. He didn't think he could make his feet walk all the way to the end where it was deeper.

His paralyzing fear of water went beyond not being a strong swimmer. One summer in England on a family holiday at the shore, he suffered a terrifying scare that ended in tragedy. His younger sister was playing in the shallows when a wave crashed on top of her, pulling her deeper into the water. Young Jonathon dove in after her and quickly became overwhelmed by the current. The only lifeguard on duty went in after Jonathon first and delivered him safely back to shore, but by the time he reached his little sister, it was too late. She couldn't be revived. The tragedy irrevocably changed his life and the dynamics of the family. In their silence, they left him to shoulder the blame. He'd never forgiven himself.

Desperate to get the ordeal over with, he called out, gesturing with his hands. "Are you going to pull around to the side?"

The captain's head popped partway through the side window. "Too shallow with the tide going out. C'mon! We're running out of time."

Reluctantly, Sterling set off down the dock, shuffling as he went, keeping an eye on the sides so he didn't venture too close to either. Walking toward the water took on a different, more terrifying feel than it did when his back was to it after he'd arrived on the seaplane, and he had the inn in his sights. His heart thumped against his ribcage as he fought back memories flashing through his head.

"Let's go. You're not my only stop. We're losing the tide," the captain barked, growing impatient, banging a hand on the side of the wheelhouse to add to the delivery's urgency.

"Okay, okay!" Sterling inched closer.

Mere steps from the boat, a swishing sound caught his attention as a thick section of rope dropped in front of him. Around his torso was a lasso, which quickly grew tighter, restricting his lung expansion. His arms were pinned to his sides. The captain gunned the engine, pulling away from the dock, yanking Sterling several feet through the air and then plunging him into the frigid water, face first. Terror ripped through his body as he was dragged, swallowing water, coughing, struggling to get his head above the surface to catch some air.

The whir of the engines wound down, slowing the boat. He felt himself being reeled through the water like the catch of the day. Just when his lungs screamed for air and he couldn't keep himself from taking a breath, his head popped out and hit something solid, suspending stars in front of his eyes. Someone grabbed him from above, from under his arms, and pulled him up over the side of the boat where he was unceremoniously dropped, sputtering and gasping for air, and left to flail around on the slippery deck, grasping for something to hang onto. Once he steadied himself, a fist landed square on his cheekbone, sending a bolt of pain exploding through his head, landing him back on the deck. He recovered and looked up into the face of the captain who removed the cap, allowing long bright red wavy hair to tumble down. Once the sunglasses came off, Sterling looked into the eyes he'd married, not two years earlier.

"Lucretia! You're okay." His lungs burned with each word. Small puffs of air were all he could manage to take in.

She removed the oversized fisherman's rain slicker, tossing it onto an overturned milk crate beneath the captain's wheel.

Realizing she'd used it to see out the front windows properly, he reprimanded himself for being duped by a pint-sized bitch who made him think she was some macho guy captaining a boat.

She wasn't fooled by his smooth tone and pleading eyes. "Don't even . . . you bastard." She leaned into the wheelhouse to cut the engines, pointed an accusatory finger at him, and took a step closer. "Did you *really* think I had cheated on you? I waited all those months for you to return. . . . Endured a goddamn Maine winter while you were away. Have you ever lived through one? Or better yet, how about a blizzard? That was the highlight. Did you so much as check in to see how I was doing? Did you have any idea it was one of the worst winters on record? You stayed away *weeks* longer than you'd planned, but I *still* waited patiently for you to return. Then you show up without so much as a 'hey I'm heading home,' and when you get here you think it's cute to surprise me, which would have been fine if you had taken a second to understand what you'd walked into."

Sterling shifted his position on the deck and Lucretia read that to mean he was trying to get up. She shoved a boot into his chest and watched with satisfaction as he fell backward.

"Your anger got the best of you. You snapped. . . . Did you really think you could get away with it?" Lucretia stepped back and folded her arms, looking for him to address her questions.

Away with *it?* She didn't know for sure what he had done. With his breathing returning to a more normal rhythm, he felt marginally stronger than when he was pulled aboard . . . by her? How did she manage that? And how dare she question how long he chose to stay away?

"You ungrateful bitch. Who are you to question how I run my business? Who do you think is funding this pet project of yours? *My* business. My *successful* business. Don't you dare question how I conduct it and how long that takes. You're here, running an inn, competing with every other lodging establishment in this archaic town. If it wasn't on the water, it would be some backwoods shit-hole—as you Americans say—that no one would ever go out of their way to visit. For God's sake, I don't know how you grew up here. There's nothing here. And the hellacious winters that go on for six months, you might as well be bears that hibernate. Why would you want to go out in the bitter cold?"

He hadn't intended to divulge how much he hated the cold and snow, but she'd pushed him there. She was also getting him off topic, too.

"I found you with him . . . because you didn't know I was near. You got bored while I was away. I know you. You get bored easily, so you decided to have some fun. And you didn't expect to be interrupted, did you?"

A larger boat passed within several yards, causing theirs to bob wildly before subsiding again.

"You were totally off base. Nothing was going on. But you couldn't help yourself, could you? Your anger got the best of you. And you went after poor Edward. Innocent Ed who—"

"Oh, he's not so innocent. I saw the look in his eye. He was guilty as hell."

"That wasn't the look of guilt. He was terrified of you. All the staff are."

"Yes! Rightfully so. He was guilty of fraternizing with my wife and got caught."

"No, he didn't, but you punished him anyway. Took care of it straight away, as you say. Didn't you?"

Lucretia was fishing, and he wasn't going to fill in the blanks for her. "Of course. I did what was necessary under the circumstances."

"So how'd you do it exactly? I was unconscious for a while, so I missed all the fun."

Sterling's insides stirred in twisted anticipation of reliving the murder. He'd surprised even himself, but he couldn't let her entice him to spill all the gory details.

"Was it your bare hands? Or did you get lucky, and he tripped and fell, taking care of the morbid task for you?"

He flared his eyes in indignation. "Oh, no. It wasn't that easy. He put up a fight, but I took him on. No one is going to sleep with my wife and get away with it."

"We didn't sleep to—"

"You know I didn't mean for you to get hurt in all this. You couldn't stay out of it. I'm sorry if you got a bump on the head in the process."

"So how did you murder him, exactly?"

"Murder, Lucretia? Such a strong word. I don't look like I could commit such an atrocity, do I? But, I suppose you never know what you're entirely capable of until the situation presents itself." It had been easy. The kid stopped breathing in no time. Jonathon was satisfied in his accomplishment, but he wasn't going to share that with her. He couldn't have her thinking of him as the monster she'd married and shared a bed with. Maybe it wasn't something to be proud of, but he didn't know he had it in him before that night.

"So what did you do with his body? Find a good hiding place for him?" The corner of her mouth curled up as if enjoying his tale.

Grinning, he was pleased she needed to know. She'd never be able to find him. Probably drive her insane thinking about it. Served her right. "Let's just say you won't be seeing his face around the inn anymore." He wasn't going to reveal where the kid was buried. No body. No evidence.

Sterling could sense someone else on the boat, close by. Out stepped a man from behind the wheelhouse with a coiled rope in hand. He didn't recognize him and figured he was merely a hired hand.

"Jonathon, I don't know if you've officially met Ben. He's the one who lassoed you off the dock. Very skillfully, I might add. Learned how to rope growing up in Montana. Nice job, Ben." She shot him an air high five.

The cowboy nodded in acknowledgment.

Sterling didn't like the way they looked at each other. If he wasn't sprawled on his ass, he'd knock the guy into next week, not just for lassoing him into the icy water but for undoubtedly having a romp in his wife's bed. *And look at the way she's parading him in front of me.* His hands curled into tight fists. Who else had she been with?

The hum of an approaching boat grew louder then quieted as it pulled up alongside to idle. The police chief swiftly hopped across onto their boat, surprisingly adept for a man his size. Eager to connect with someone who could help him and was paid to do so, Sterling sprang to his feet but found a revolver pointing at his nose once he managed to get upright.

"And now you'll pay for what you've done," Lucretia assured him.

Maintaining his innocence, he shifted gears and his tone of voice. "Afternoon, Mack."

"Don't bother with the false pretenses, Sterling. We not only heard every word, we recorded it." He nodded toward Ben who held up his cell. "You've got a long list of charges hanging around your neck. Just wish I could tack on a charge for being an outsider who never tried to fit in. You've always been way overdressed for these parts. Us Mainers aren't as tight-assed as you. You stick out with your expensive, custom-tailored suits." He flicked the edge of Sterling's lapel, flipping it up onto his neck.

"Now we're going to take a little ride back to the dock, and I get to take you in. So go ahead and sit down. Might as well make yourself comfortable. Probably be a long time before you'll get the chance again."

Lucretia fired up the engines and eased the throttle forward, turning the boat back around toward shore. An officer on harbor patrol's boat led the way.

With his back against the wall, nowhere to turn, and an almost certain conviction looming, Sterling looked for a way out. He wasn't going to jail for something he didn't deserve. He'd lose everything—everything he'd worked so hard for. It was all slipping through his fingers. He'd never be able to face his brothers.

He found his out when they neared Cuckholds Light. He'd been behaving the entire trip back in, sitting quietly at the stern, slumped in the corner looking defeated; the chief hadn't bothered with cuffs. So they didn't expect him to hop off the back of the boat when they had their heads turned. He seized the opportunity, steering clear of the two large, rumbling engines churning up the ocean.

CHAPTER NINETEEN

Fingering *the skeleton key,* turning it over and over in her palm, Elizabeth surveyed the room she'd shared with her pup during the weekend. What else could it possibly open? Her eyes traveled to the top of the antique bureau. Along the top were three narrow drawers, each with a tarnished knob and a lock centered above it.

The one on the left opened easily to reveal an old pipe and leather bag with a faint smell of tobacco. The middle one contained an accordion-style paper fan with faded mauve flowers. The drawer on the far right held an envelope with no notations on the outside.

Elizabeth slipped a handwritten note out of the envelope that read:

> My dear sweet daughter, Lucretia,
>   If I am not able to tell you myself, my hopes are that you will lay your eyes on this

letter because there is something I must tell you even if it is from beyond the grave.

My love for you (and your father's as well) cannot be measured. I (we) love you more than you can imagine. And you won't be able to understand until you have your own child and I pray that someday you will be blessed with a beautiful child of your own.

Some would say that a biological mother's love is stronger than an adoptive mother's. I vehemently disagree. In some cases an adoptive mother's love may be stronger. Perhaps I can lay claim to that.

Lord knows we tried and tried for years to have a child on our own and it just wasn't meant to be. I learned later that after all those years that I was given arsenic as a child to help "build me up," it turns out it was more detrimental than productive. At the time it was believed to be similar to what would now be an iron supplement. Day after day, my mother added two to three drops into my milk or juice, thinking it was helping me. I had been riddled with a frail body which was cause for constant concern for my parents. So when the doctor recommended giving me a couple drops of arsenic to help my body become stronger like my classmates, they eagerly bought the small brown bottle with the eyedropper stopper. They only wanted what was best for me. Turns out it made me sterile.

After trying all those years and being distraught with disappointment, we were blessed to be able to adopt you. A sweet six pound, nine ounce baby girl who was barely two weeks old. It was almost too good to be true. And you arrived in April so it was completely believable that we had conceived late summer and by the time I would have been showing, we were in the throes of a nasty Maine winter with a blizzard thrown in to add to the snowfall and difficulty to navigate around town. I didn't venture out much. So by the time everyone dug themselves out of the snowdrifts, we had a precious baby girl to show off.

You were absolutely beautiful (And continue to be, inside and out.). Some people asked about your stunning red hair and where it came from. After all, neither your father nor I had anything resembling the luscious color of your locks. It was incredible to feast our eyes on. So unusual. But genetics was on our side. Apparently red hair, and yours is a stunning shade, is a recessive trait. Someone can carry the trait without exhibiting it. So it was certainly feasible that a daughter of ours could have red hair. I think I had an uncle with red hair. Maybe even a mustache to go with it. You fit right into our family and we were tickled you had arrived. I think we loved you before we set eyes on you.

We also love the young woman you've grown into. We couldn't be prouder. We will love you always. In life and afterwards. Follow your dreams. Stay true to yourself. Know that you will always be in our hearts.

Love you, Lucretia.

Mom & Dad

Struggling to suppress a click in her throat, Elizabeth doubted Lucretia knew the letter existed. She refolded it and slipped it back inside the envelope, securing the drawer with the key. A small wicker trash can on the floor to the side of the dresser contained some sort of fabric she hadn't noticed before. She fished out a couple pillowcases, puzzled as to why they were there, and tossed them back in again.

CHAPTER TWENTY

With the skeleton key pressed into her palm, she couldn't resist the idea of finding out if there was anything else it would open on the property. Her first stop would be the cottages. Sea Glass and Sandpiper looked to have been occupied during the weekend as evidenced by the unmade beds, but the guests had cleared out, presumably after the police had cleared them from the investigation. She tried the key in each one, but it wouldn't turn in either lock. Farther into the woods, Water's Edge and Sea Breeze appeared to be unoccupied, as their renovations were incomplete. Paint cans and tarps littered the floor where they'd been left on Friday afternoon.

Heading down the path, Elizabeth came upon Sebago, tucked the deepest among the trees, which also appeared to be in the midst of a redo. Upon closer inspection, it looked like there was a blanket scrunched up on the bed in the middle of the floor where it had been pushed away from the walls that were getting painted.

Elizabeth tried the key. It resisted at first and then turned with a clunk. Pushing her way into the room, she noticed something purple sticking out from under the pillow and lifted the edge of the case. A velvet drawstring bag from a whiskey bottle. Did it belong to Sterling? Whiskey seemed to be his liquor of choice. It was the first thing he'd offered the chief on his return to the inn. Or could it be Ben's? As a bartender, he would have access to all sorts of alcohol-related paraphernalia.

The bag was cinched tightly at the top, and it took a moment of wriggling and wedging a finger down into the small opening before she was able to pry it open. It was filled with antique buttons; metal filigreed and tarnished with age, abalone shell that shimmered in the daylight, colorful enamel that was chipped in places, and crystal-encrusted that had lost their luster. Turning the bag upside down, she dumped the contents, watching the buttons bounce off the bedding, colliding with each other. As they tumbled, one item stood out from the rest. It wasn't a button. It had an entirely different shape. It was small key. But not a skeleton key. It was brass and more modern. She scooped it up and tried to make out the words stamped on it. Brushing her thumb across the accumulated film of dirt she examined it more closely. "Rand Leopold" it read in uneven type. The name sounded familiar. She considered it carefully, finally deciding it was the name of a furniture company. One of the pieces in the carriage house loft? She tucked it securely into her pocket.

Gathering up the loose buttons and re-cinching the bag, she tucked it back under the blanket.

Armed with the newfound key, Elizabeth's curiosity drew her back to the carriage house.

She slipped into the darkened corner where the ladder led to the loft. Curious for one more look, she had to find out if her cottage find fit one of the pieces tucked out of sight. Scampering to the top, she scrambled over the edge and headed for the desk.

Sliding the key into the slot, she turned it. With few soft surfaces to dampen the sound, the click echoed. The rolltop slid easily but didn't reveal anything other than the beautiful polished wood interior; empty slots waiting for mail or private notes to be slipped inside, narrow drawers that could hold personalized stationery, and miniature doors with tiny knobs that beckoned to be opened. Were there secret compartments behind them? One tug and antique silverware spilled out with a clang and thud onto the desktop. She picked up a knife and examined the detail. The unmistakable letter L was engraved on each one. What was the Livingston silver doing in the loft?

Next she went for the drawers on either side of the chair opening. One by one she pulled on the handles but to no avail. Yet there were no keyholes to access. She ran her finger along the edge of the top middle drawer and all the way to the back where her finger caught on a latch sticking out. She pulled it and released the drawers on one side so they swung open as a unit. Inside was a painting in an ornate gold frame with a familiar signature. A Pissarro. She repeated the steps for the other side. The latch released the opposite set of drawers to reveal another painting she recognized as a Manet.

"What have you found, Elizabeth?"

Startled, she pivoted on her heals, flailing to catch her balance. "Ana."

"You're the last person I expected to find nosing around up here."

"Just following up on a hunch." Elizabeth wondered what Ana was doing in the loft.

"A hunch?"

"Yeah, I found this key and thought I knew what it went to. Sure enough, it did. It's such a beautiful old desk. You don't see many of these anymore." She closed the two doors with gentle hands. "The Leopold Company only manufactured these beauties until around the early 1900s. It's gorgeous. Love all the compartments." Her nerves caused her to rattle on incessantly. She stroked the edges of the desk in an attempt to convince Ana of her infatuation with the piece.

"How do you know about antiques? Are you in the business?"

"Oh, no. I mean, I've had plenty of clients in my interior design career who owned phenomenal pieces, but my grandmother had a desk exactly like this. As a young girl I loved to poke around in it, looking for secret compartments, until someone came along and shooed me away."

"Well, maybe someone should shoo you away from here. How did you know it was up here?"

Puzzled, Elizabeth couldn't understand why she was acting so belligerently. In Chauncey's, Ana had asked for her help out of concern for Lucretia.

"Why the hostile behavior? I'm on your side, remember? You *are* aware your friend is fine and no longer missing, aren't you? At least, that's the word around the inn."

Ignoring the question, Ana slipped between Elizabeth and the desk.

"What are you hiding?" Then she remembered the bedroll. "Who are you protecting?" Had she seen Elizabeth scale the ladder to the loft and followed her?

Ana smirked as though she had intimate knowledge.

"Do you know who's been sleeping here?" Elizabeth pressed further.

"Not much sleeping goes on there." She nodded toward the desk.

Elizabeth looked to her for more. "Who? . . . Is it Ben? And someone from the inn? . . . Lucretia?"

Bursting into a guffaw, Ana quieted back down as if out of concern for being overheard. "Oh no, it's not Ben. And if it was, he certainly wouldn't be with her."

"How do you know?"

Ana paused, perhaps deciding whether she should confide in an outsider.

"Because she and I are lovers."

Considering her revelation, if Sterling suspected their relationship, that would explain why he had a strong distaste for Ana.

"I see." Elizabeth strained not to react outwardly.

"And I'm the only one who can call her Lucy."

"Why is that?"

Ana beamed with a coy smirk. "Because I'm the only one she lets in. She's been through a great deal of pain in her life and has built up an emotional barrier to protect herself. She keeps everyone out—emotionally—except me. She can only allow one person to get close to her at a time. And Lucy is the nickname her father called her."

Chatter outside the carriage house doors drew the attention away from their conversation and the discoveries in the loft.

Another long day had slipped away, and Elizabeth was discouraged to still be at the inn with few answers. She took Buddy to the backyard for a trot around the property before they turned in for the night. One more stroll through the manicured garden would be good for both of them.

This time it had more of a desolate feel to it than when it was set up for the ceremony. The white chairs had been folded and left leaning up against the back wall of the inn. The altar still stood as a stark reminder of a wedding that never took place.

Buddy's curious nose led them across the yard and up the crumbling stone steps to the family cemetery where Elizabeth came to a halt. It looked nothing like the last time they'd seen it. Someone had been busy. Sod lay haphazardly. A wooden-handled shovel stuck out of a large pile of light sandy dirt. As they crept closer, the overgrown grasses tickled her ankles. The graves on the far side of the cemetery, the oldest in the plot, had been violated. Dirt packed into mounds gave the impression someone had been recently buried—or re-buried.

Who could have done such a thing? What monster would desecrate the final resting spot of the Livingston family ancestors? Was it vandalism, or were they after something specific? It turned her stomach to think someone could dig up a coffin and open it. Were they looking for something left inside? The buttons she'd found in the cottage? Someone had a disturbing agenda.

Suddenly aware Buddy's wagging tail was sticking out of the bushes nearby, she tore herself away from the gruesome images she'd conjured in her mind and went in after him.

"What'd you find, Bud?"

She tugged at his collar, but he wouldn't budge. Pulling aside a thick branch, she noticed a weathered box with a lid. The keyhole looked similar to the one on the door to her room.

"Could it?" she wondered aloud. "One way to find out."

Hauling the heavy box out of the bushes far enough to tilt it open, she slid the fragile metal key into the slot, turning it slowly with a click.

"No way." Lifting the lid, she peered in to find a few pieces of antique jewelry, pocket watches, and spectacles scattered in the bottom of it. Someone was just getting started.

"The police will want to know about this, Buddy." He wagged his back end, pleased with himself.

Unsure how this and all the other pieces fit together, she questioned the sense of remaining at the inn any longer. If she passed along her findings, surely the authorities would straighten it all out. Or would they? And what of Rashelle's disappearance? No one seemed to know her or her whereabouts. Torn between her loyalty to her friend and the urgency to return to Connecticut to service her clients, Elizabeth resigned herself to leaving the search in—what she hoped were—the capable hands of local law enforcement. She'd catch up with the chief in the morning. They were staying their last night at the inn.

CHAPTER TWENTY-ONE

With check-out time looming, Elizabeth was none too sorry to leave the inn behind, lamenting ever having set foot inside. Their weekend away had regrettably turned into three days, keeping her from client work longer than she would have liked. The only upside was the Monday morning traffic wouldn't be bad. Tourists traveling into or out of the state usually trekked on Fridays and Sundays.

After making a trip to her car to stow their luggage behind the seats, she stopped by the front desk to turn in the skeleton key. The young girl behind the desk hesitated before taking it from her.

"Excuse me, what does this go to?"

"My room. The room I stayed in this weekend."

She rotated it in her fingers, examining the worn curved edges and intricate cutouts.

"I . . . I've never seen anything like this. What room did you say you were in?"

"I didn't, but it was 213."

"I don't understand. That—"

"Leaving so soon?"

A woman with fiery red hair, partially tamed in a loose French braid off-center, appeared from behind. A white gauze bandage partially covered the side of her forehead. Eyes that held the sadness of untold pain went to the key dangling in the clerk's fingers. "Where did that come from?" She snatched it from her and concealed it in a tight fist.

"Oh, you must be Lucretia." Elizabeth recognized her from Florence's description.

"Yes, I am."

"So good to meet you. I'm Elizabeth Pennington." Lucretia had to switch the key to the other hand in order to shake.

Elizabeth jumped to the clerk's rescue. "That was my room key. I was in 213."

Visibly rattled, Lucretia finally found words. "We *never* give out this key. No one *ever* goes in that room."

"I'm so sorry. This is the key I was given when I—"

"Who?—Who gave it to you?" Lucretia demanded, putting Elizabeth on the defensive.

"Whoever was on duty Friday night when I got here. . . . Chip? I think his name was Chip. He apologized he wasn't familiar with the check-in process because it wasn't his usual job." She regretted mentioning Chip's name, fearful she'd implicated him unnecessarily.

"That was my mother's room," her voice trailed off.

"Lucretia, I'm so sorry. I had no idea. If I had, I certainly wouldn't have—"

Showing her palm, she softened. "No worries. She probably wouldn't have minded. Let's move on. Tell me you have time to join me for breakfast before you take off," she implored, gesturing toward the front of the inn.

Speaking directly to the clerk, Lucretia assured her she would handle the check-out later.

A bit surprised by the invite but not having the heart to refuse, Elizabeth acquiesced and followed her into the drawing room with Buddy at her heels. There, a table was laid out with hot food in covered chafing dishes, platters of pasties and rolls, and a tiered stand with pieces of whole fruit and biscotti—a feast Pennington Point Inn would have been proud of. In the center of the spread was a Wedgewood vase with a stunning arrangement of summer blooms reminiscent of Elizabeth's grandmother's floral displays, particularly the one in the inn's foyer that greeted guests upon their arrival.

As they pulled together a light meal for themselves, Lizzi noticed a black and white photograph in an antique filigree frame on the wall behind the table. She recognized the subject as the woman who had rescued Buddy when he'd gotten loose at the historical society and brought him back to her. She inquired who she was but had a feeling she knew.

"That's my mother. My father took that photo the summer before my senior year of college. We were at a local fundraiser. . . . Ya know, she loved the town's Victorian Days. She loved to dress up in the long dresses and big floppy hats. She practically had a closet full to choose from. It was as if she'd been born in the wrong century." She chuckled to herself. "Oh, and you must try the blueberry crisp. It's made with wild Maine blueberries—canned from last summer, but still delicious."

Slow to process the confirmation of her inkling, Elizabeth could only mutter, "What a pleasant memory that must be for you."

Once they settled into a corner next to the fireplace on the far side of the room, Lucretia laid her plate down on the low table between them with the skeleton key alongside it and leaned forward as if she had no intention of eating.

"I have to apologize. Apparently when you arrived someone gave you the key to a room we haven't used in years."

That would explain the mustiness and the dated furnishings. And why housekeeping never entered the room to tidy up.

"In fact we haven't handed out those old keys in a very long time." Her voice quieted. "They tend to open more than just the lock they were intended to open," she confided.

Amused Lucretia would reveal such a thing to her, Elizabeth offered, "The room was . . . quaint. Loved the French doors and Juliet balconies looking out onto the gardens."

"It was actually my parents' room. My mother loved that view, too. My father never could understand why she wouldn't want a harbor view across the hall, but she didn't grow up on the sea. He did. After they passed away I didn't have the heart to change anything in it. It was in that room that Jonathon walked in on me the other night. Talking. I was just talking with one of our staff. He showed up unannounced. He got the wrong idea and went nuts. Jumped to conclusions." She clamped her eyes shut in a painful grimace.

"I'm so sorry for what you've been through, now and years ago when your parents—"

Lifting her hand off her lap as if to stop her new friend before she disinterred long-since buried pain and suffering, Lucretia dismissed the topic.

"It's unfortunate we didn't get a chance to meet formally and get to know one another under different circumstances."

"Yes, that certainly would have been nice." Lizzi wondered if Ana'd had a hand in their chance meeting.

"Miss Livingston?" Addressing her boss by her maiden name, Juanita poked her head in, clearly not expecting to see Lucretia, and darted across the room. "Are you all right? I was so worried about you." She leaned in closer than one would expect an employee to do.

Lucretia gently took hold of Juanita's upper arm with splayed fingers like a mother keeping a child close in order to talk earnestly with her. "I'm sorry I worried you so. Thanks for keeping your word. That meant the world to me."

"Of course. What happened to you? Are you all right? I thought the worst when you didn't come back." She reached out but stopped short of making contact with Lucretia's bandage.

"Oh, this?" She brushed an errant strand of hair from her forehead. "It's nothing. Really. Just a small cut after I fell down the stairs. Didn't even need stitches."

"*Fell* down the—" Juanita glanced to Elizabeth and didn't finish her thought.

"I'm fine. Really. Thanks so much for everything you've done for me. I appreciate it." With that, she hugged the housekeeper, sending her on her way, and then flopped back into the wingback.

"You know, my mother always used to tell me that everything happens for a reason . . . that we're supposed to learn lessons from what we have to deal with in life. Right now, I'm hard-pressed to figure out a lesson in any of this." Her hand went to her recent wound and fingered the corners of the bandage.

Elizabeth remained silent, unable to put words together that reflected her genuine empathy for her yet didn't sound contrived. The two women shared the unenviable bond of losing both parents in a single tragic event. While Lucretia had been able to share her first twenty years with hers and all the memories created in that time, the pain from losing them must have been excruciatingly vivid. The tragedy surrounding Elizabeth's mother and father happened at such a young age, her memory of them was fuzzy, and she would have given anything to have had them as long as Lucretia had her parents. Elizabeth fought to push away her irrational envy.

Vibrating in her pocket stirred Lucretia. She excused herself when she checked the caller ID, scooting to the edge of the chair.

"Hey, Mack." Her eyes traveled the length of the dark wallpaper to a window looking out to the harbor. "Did you find anything yet?" She bit her lower lip, squinting slightly as she listened. "I see. That's interesting. He covered some miles, didn't he?" Lucretia brushed aside a stubborn red tendril and chuckled. "All right. Well, I appreciate you calling. Sorry for the dirty work. . . . Okay. Glad to know—" With her elbow dug into the arm of the chair, she rested her head on her free hand. "Thank you, I appreciate that. What's that? . . . No, I haven't seen Ben since yesterday morning. . . . Okay. Thanks."

Tossing her cell onto the smooth wooden table, it slid halfway across and struck the key, sending it over the edge closest to Elizabeth. Puzzled at first, she thought Lucretia intended for her to pick up the phone to speak with the chief but then realized she'd ended the call.

"They found the bastard."

"Who?"

"Jonathon."

"Jonathon?"

"Yeah, you may not have heard the sordid details, but the police were after him and caught up to him by boat. He was so desperate he jumped off the back of it when he was in custody."

"What?"

"Yeah, pretty stupid. He couldn't swim well, and he was also fully clothed."

Retrieving the key from under her chair, Elizabeth rolled it in her palms like a pair of dice. Unless Lucretia specifically asked for it back, she'd hang onto it for a while longer. "So Chief Mack thinks he found him?"

"Yeah, the current carried him all the way down to Popham Beach. A couple out on a walk with their dog this morning found him washed up on shore."

She sunk back into her chair and wrapped herself with her arms. "Good God . . . what a way to go. Those poor people. He must have been quite a mess to set their sights on. And rather ironic, since he had such a fear of water. He was so desperate, he saw that as his only way out."

"I'm sorry, Lucretia. How awful."

The newly widowed innkeeper remained silent and tucked her legs beneath her. It looked like the chair was swallowing her petite frame.

"Can't believe he shoved me down the stairs and—"

"He didn't." Elizabeth's dislike for the man shifted toward hatred.

"Yes, he did. But he didn't stick around to find out how badly I was hurt, so I took off and got as far away from him as I could and then let him wonder. Probably drove him nuts."

"When did that happen? Was anyone else around?"

"Wednesday evening. There were no staff here except for Ed. Oh, and Juanita. I don't think Jonathon saw her. She was so upset. Heard the commotion and came running. There was blood everywhere. Head wounds tend to look worse than they really are, though. I left him to clean it all up. We weren't open yet. Still wrapping up last-minute details. And we were really only opening up for the wedding. *His* wedding. We were happy to do that for someone who has been such a loyal employee. God, I can't believe how it all turned out."

"Wednesday evening? How is that possible? I watched Sterling arrive on a seaplane Saturday afternoon after the ceremony was called off."

"They're still trying to figure out his movements after that evening. There were plenty of witnesses that say they saw him arrive by seaplane as you did. But he was definitely here before that and staged his arrival. I suppose he figured it would be his word against mine, and if I had a bump on the head from 'falling' down the stairs, I wouldn't be a reliable witness."

"Where did you go?"

"At first, I was just running. So scared. I caught up with Ben, who was nice enough to let me hide out on his boat."

CHAPTER TWENTY-ONE

"The *Selma Ann?*"

"Yes."

"It's not really *his* boat." Elizabeth couldn't resist pointing out the clarification.

"It's not really *anyone's* boat," Lucretia retorted. "It's there for anyone who needs to use it for a while. That's what old Mr. Stiles would have wanted. He had a heart of gold. Very giving. After his wife passed away he sold most of his belongings and his beautiful home up on the hill and moved onto the *Selma Ann.*"

"So you hid out there leaving everyone to wonder what happened to you." Elizabeth immediately regretted her words sounded so accusatory.

"I think the only one who was really concerned was Jonathon, and he deserved it. He left me at the bottom of the stairs in a bloody heap. Poor Juanita. I told her to stay out of it and keep it to herself. She didn't want to, but I made her promise. I think she's afraid of him."

Elizabeth could understand why.

"I bet he wondered if he'd killed me. He left me there and went back to the room where he'd left Ed. God, I had no idea what he'd done to him. That animal. Who knew what he was capable of?"

"You didn't?"

"Of course not. Then again, we don't know *exactly* what he did. Jonathon stopped short of giving us all the details. If I had known about his extreme anger and jealousy, I never would have married him. . . . I wish I hadn't." She gazed out the front windows to the calming view of the harbor before continuing. "Ever think you've fallen in love with someone only to have him turn out different than you thought he was?"

"Not exactly."

"Ever fallen in love?"

Elizabeth's cheeks flushed. They were entering uncharted territory, her uncomfortable zone where she had very little experience. "Well, last summer I met this guy that I fell for. We kind of went our separate ways at the end of the summer though. I'm surprised by how often I think of him." Her thoughts returned to the evening she'd first arrived back at her family's inn and was introduced to the recently hired tennis pro, amused at the tickle in her abdomen.

"You should track him down."

Elizabeth dismissed the idea with her hand.

"No, really. You should have seen how your face lit up when you started talking about him. What's his name?"

"His name? Uh . . . Kurt."

"Well, I think you should find a way to reconnect with him. He's probably thinking of you as often as you think of him."

"Oh, I don't know. . . ."

"Seriously, they say when you think of someone out of the blue, it's because they're thinking about you. It makes sense."

"We'll see. But I doubt it. A long time has passed and I haven't heard from him."

"Maybe he doesn't think you're interested. You seem like you wouldn't exactly divulge all your intimate thoughts and feelings. He may have no idea."

Anxious to get off the topic, Elizabeth steered Lucretia back to her situation.

"So what was it like to hang out on the *Selma Ann?* Tight quarters, I bet. You were fortunate to be able to take refuge there."

"Absolutely. Of course, when the boat got loose from its mooring the other morning, my secret was almost common knowledge, but I got that straightened out quickly. So, yeah, I was quite fortunate to have that. I'm not sure what I would have done otherwise."

"Stay with Ana?"

"Oh no! I thought of that. She was the first person I thought of, but I didn't want to put her in danger. That would have been the first place he would have looked for me . . . if he looked. Who knows what he would have done. He hates her. It was better to keep Ana out of it. Thank God for Ben. He was such a gentleman and went to stay with a friend, so I could have my privacy on the boat."

"With a friend? That was nice."

"Yeah."

"Any chance he would have come here? Stayed in the carriage house loft? Or the cottages?"

"I suppose it's possible. . . . He did mention he snuck into the cellar and stayed there during the winter months."

"Are you aware that there are those in town who think Ben had something to do with your parents' deaths?"

"Careful who you listen to, Elizabeth. Don't pay any attention to that kind of talk. You can't lose sleep over what some narrow-minded local is speculating and blabbing about at the pub. They've got nothing better to do. It's pathetic. They need to mind their own business. The rumors that get started around here . . ."

The two sat in silence until Lucretia picked up her plate as if to start in on her breakfast only to deposit it on her lap. "Guess the staff won't miss Jonathon. I don't think any of them particularly cared for him. He scared most of them."

"Speaking of staff, I hope you don't mind me asking about a friend of mine who came to work here recently. I haven't been able to reach her all weekend and I'm rather worried. It was a last-minute decision to come up for the wedding, and I thought it would be fun to surprise her. At first, when she didn't answer her phone, I figured she was out for the evening. It was Friday night. But as the weekend went on, I had a harder time coming up with a logical explanation why she wasn't picking up. Now I'm really concerned."

"Who's your friend?"

"Your new day manager. Rashelle."

"Rashelle," she repeated, looking contemplative.

"I know her as Shelle, but I think you might call her Shelly."

"Oh, Shelly! Shelly Pedersen. Yes, she just started at the front desk. Isn't it funny that you know her, too?"

"What did you say her last name is?" Elizabeth leaned forward.

"Pedersen."

"Not Harper? Rashelle Harper?" She endeavored to keep her voice even. *How could that be?*

"No. And I think Shelly's full name is Michelle."

Elizabeth struggled to form words to express the extent of her bewilderment. "I'm sorry. There must be some sort of mix-up."

Sliding her cell out of her pocket, she grew more anxious to reach her friend. Willing Rashelle to pick up at the other end, against what seemed like impossible odds, she jolted upright with the click in her ear.

"Yeah!" The voice was rough and gravelly, like she'd been rudely awakened in the middle of the night.

"Shelle, is that you?"

"Yeah, what's up girl?" Her words faded away into a cough and throat clearing.

"Where've you been? I've been trying to reach you all weekend." Elizabeth wanted to smack the indifference right out of her.

"Sorry, I got tied up. Couldn't get to my phone."

"Tied up? What's that supposed to mean? I drove all the way up to Maine to surprise you and then couldn't reach you." The fact that the wedding was the true catalyst for her making the trip was irrelevant at the moment. "I left messages and kept calling after your voicemail filled up. Where the hell *are* you?"

"You're in Maine?" Rashelle perked up.

"Yes, where are *you*?"

Silence on the other end.

"Shelle!"

"I'm here, Lizzi. Take it easy. I spent the weekend in a wine cellar. I'm feelin' kinda crappy."

"You've been drinking for three days? Geez Shelle, that's a record, even for you."

"No, I wasn't drinking. Although I thought about it the entire time. If I'd had a corkscrew, that would have—"

"*What* are you talking about, Rashelle? Damn it, you're not making any sense."

"I got locked in the f**king wine cellar on Friday afternoon after everyone else had left. The door shut behind me when I was shelving some wine bottles that just couldn't wait 'til Monday.

Although I swear someone did it to me on purpose. . . . I'd left my phone sitting on the counter in the kitchen so I couldn't do anything except wait for someone to show up and let me out."

"Where? What wine cellar?"

"At the inn."

"What inn?"

"Lizzi, what do you mean? I told you I got a job at Boothbay Inn."

"Yeah, well, I'm there now and have been all weekend and you're not—"

"How is that possible? We haven't opened yet. That's why I had to wait until this morning to get out. I look and feel absolutely disgusting—wait a minute. Are you at The Inn on Boothbay *Harbor*? On the water? On Grandview Avenue?"

"Yes, and you're not anywhere in sight. What's going on?" Had her friend lied about getting the job? Was she embarrassed to admit she still hadn't landed anything? "Why would you tell me you're—"

"Well that's because I'm at Boothbay Inn. The next town over. In Boothbay. Not Boothbay Harbor. You're at The Inn *on* Boothbay *Harbor*."

Elizabeth let her cell drop into her lap. *How could she have been so stupid?* She should have caught that subtle yet critical distinction. Lucretia looked to her for an explanation from across the table. Holding her off for the moment with a raised finger, Lizzi snatched up her phone again.

"Rashelle, I'm sorry. It's my mistake. I should have known. And I'm sorry you had to spend the weekend in the cellar. I thought the worst, but I'm glad you're okay."

"I don't know that I would say I'm okay, but I'll live. Look, I'm going to crash for a while. Catch up on some sleep. In my own bed instead of perched on the rickety wooden stairs in a musty old wine cellar. Maybe we can grab a drink later."

"All right, Shelle. Sounds good. Get some rest. Call me later." Elizabeth signed off and tucked her cell in her palm.

"Your friend has resurfaced?" The corner of Lucretia's mouth turned up in amusement.

"Yeah, it was a simple misunderstanding." Elizabeth was not about to go into all the embarrassing details. She was ready to move on. "So back to more serious matters. . . . What's ahead for you?"

Lucretia remained silent as if she hadn't heard the question.

"I'm sorry. That was too personal. You don't have to—"

"Not at all." She pushed aside her apology with a flick of her hand. "It's a fair question. I guess I'll go back to what I was doing before Jonathon stumbled into my life—or more accurately, stampeded. I'm not sure our marriage would have lasted much longer anyway, given where we were headed. . . . I'll run the inn the way I see fit without his intrusions." She scanned the room. "Maybe I'll redecorate, and this time I'll do it in the style I wanted. Not so damn masculine." Running her fingers down the arm of the chair, Lucretia peeled up the end of the protective sleeve. "I mean, who uses these arm caps anymore?" She stripped it off and tossed it onto a nearby sofa. "God, he had awful taste. It was like he was trying to turn the entire inn into a man cave. Ya know, statistics say that 80 percent of the time it's the woman who makes the decision of where to stay when couples go on vacation. This place looks like he was trying to scare them off. I've got a lot of work to do, don't I? To undo everything he's done here."

"That would be quite an undertaking. And you're just getting the inn back open after being closed for renovations." Not wanting to be responsible for putting a foolish idea in Lucretia's head, Lizzi did her best to backpedal, but it didn't look like she was listening.

"It would be good to erase any evidence of his existence. It would help me forget he ever happened to me."

The sudden vibration of Lucretia's cell on the table startled them. She reached over and hit the button to answer and put it on speaker.

"What's up, Chief?"

"Lucretia, I'd like to take a look at what might be underneath the floor of the carriage house."

"And how would you do that?"

"I'm outside the inn, and I've got men standing by with ground-penetrating radar equipment. Brought them in from Augusta." He sounded proud of his accomplishment. "And, with your permission, I'd like to give them the go-ahead to get to work."

"So you brought in the men and the equipment and *then* you ask my permission?" Lucretia winked with an impish grin.

Background noise was all that emanated from the phone speaker. Lucretia laughed.

"I'm just ribbing you, Mack. Of course you've got my permission. What are you expecting to find?" Her sense of humor faded with her question.

Elizabeth recalled how Buddy lay down in the carriage house with his nose to a specific spot on the dirt floor, not wanting to leave, drawing on his training as a search and rescue dog.

"I have a gut feeling. . . . I hope I'm wrong."

Lucretia considered his request. "That's fine."

"Okay, and let me ask you this: Did you have plans to pour a concrete floor there?"

"A concrete floor? In the carriage house?"

"Yeah."

"No. Why would we do that?" Lucretia asked, scrunching up her forehead.

"I've got a truck driver standing next to me. He's driving a cement mixer filled with concrete."

"Whaaat?"

"Says he has orders to pour a floor."

Her eyes grew wide. "*Jonathon.*"

"Sounds like it. All right, I'll tell him to take his concrete elsewhere."

Muffled background noise spewed from the table while Mack dismissed the driver who understandably pushed back. What was he going to do with a truck full of cement? It wasn't the chief's problem.

Back on the line, he had a final thought. "Oh, and Lucretia, someone found an abandoned bike belonging to the inn over in East Boothbay. We figure he must have biked over there early Saturday morning where he hooked up with the seaplane operator. Apparently did it with a full suit on."

CHAPTER TWENTY-TWO

Buddy had been more than patient about being cooped up in the room at times throughout the weekend, remaining quiet beyond what Elizabeth thought he was capable of. It was time to get him out of there and hit the road. They'd had the misfortune of getting wrapped up in the sad affairs at the inn, but the authorities seemed to have things under control as much as they were going to. And although it didn't turn out like she'd pictured, she'd tracked down her friend Rashelle.

Outside, she allowed Buddy to run off leash with her running to keep up. He bounded for the manicured gardens behind the inn where he idled here and there to mark his spot. Elizabeth wandered over to the carriage house where both sets of doors were wide open, enabling her to see through the cavernous space to the harbor beyond. The old sleigh and the rest of the contents were lined up neatly outside like a used car lot. The chief and a couple men were conversing on the front lawn with their backs to her, perhaps discussing their approach to using the radar equipment. Mack interrupted their conversation to answer his cell.

"Are you sure? Oh good God, please tell me you're not serious. So he still must be out there somewhere. Just hasn't shown up on a beach yet. There haven't been any sightings in town or anywhere nearby, have there?" He paused to listen. "Goddamn it. . . . This is the last thing I want to have to tell her. All right. Thanks for letting me know. Stay on it and get back to me with anything else you find out."

Elizabeth had stepped into the shadows, to listen to the one-sided conversation. A thud on the opposite side of the carriage house suggested his fist or some other part of his body found the wall in frustration. Before long he was back on the phone again.

"Yes, Lucretia, it's Mack. I need to ask you about Jonathon's height and weight. . . . I need to verify . . . I see. Okay. Well, I'm afraid I, uh . . . I have some not-so-good news. . . . I'm sorry to have to tell you that when I told you earlier Sterling had washed up on Popham Beach, I was making an assumption. I assumed it was him because I wasn't aware of anyone else that was missing. Turns out there was a lobster boat that ran into engine problems yesterday and took on water, and the captain wasn't heard from after the original mayday—" He pulled the phone away from his ear and closed his eyes before replacing it. "Look, I'm sorry. I can't tell you how sorry I—" He removed the phone again, holding it out in front of him, and then jammed it into his pocket. Snatching his cap off his head, he ran his fingers through his thinning gray-streaked hair and slapped it back on again.

With her gut aching for Lucretia, Elizabeth slipped from her hiding spot out into the garden in time to see Buddy bounding up the steps to the cemetery. She set out in his direction on a dead run. She wasn't going to lose him again.

"Damn it, Buddy. What is it about this place that fascinates you?" She grabbed him just inside the cemetery grounds. "It's a large property with plenty of other places to explore, yet you choose this. Can't we explore over this way?" She tugged on his collar but he pulled back, her fingers slipping from her grip. She lunged and got him back under control. "That's it, I've had enough of this place. We're outta here."

They reached the car with her winded and the pup wagging his tail, looking eager to keep playing. She opened the passenger side door, but he only got as far as propping his front paws on the running board. He looked up at her as if asking with his sweet brown eyes if she was serious.

"That looks like a fun car to drive," Lucretia called from behind her, sitting up high in a late-model bright white Land Rover.

Proudly, Elizabeth admitted, "Yeah, it is. Not that I have far to commute to work. In fact, I could walk, but it makes trips like coming up here more enjoyable." She approached Lucretia's car.

Leaning out the window, she asked, "Wanna take a ride?"

Anxious to start her long drive back to Connecticut, she hesitated, glancing back at Buddy.

"He can come, too," Lucretia coaxed, reaching out and brushing the hair from Elizabeth's forehead. "I'd love your company."

She considered Ana's confession in the loft and questioned Lucretia's intentions.

"I might need your help, too."

Always a sucker for someone who declared they needed help, Elizabeth asked, "Okay, what's up?"

"Hop in. I'll show you."

As they headed down the harbor road, Elizabeth admired the sun sparkling on the water and the beautiful old homes as they passed by.

"So where we going?"

"I need to take a ride over to East Boothbay. I want to check something out." She wasn't forthcoming with any more details.

"Lucretia, I couldn't help overhearing the chief's conversation when he called to tell you it wasn't really Jonathon they'd found on the beach. I'm so sorry to hear that." For a fleeting moment Elizabeth wondered if she should be sorry for that. Did Lucretia have any lingering feelings for him?

"Oh, it doesn't surprise me in the least. He had on a suit when he jumped overboard, for Christ's sake. And I don't mean a Speedo. And wing tips, too. I'd be surprised if he made it fifty yards. No way. He wasn't a good swimmer anyway, but he couldn't make it with all that on. He's at the bottom of the harbor right now. Fish food."

"Really."

"Ay-uh."

Elizabeth was pleased to hear Lucretia's Maine upbringing shining through. It reminded her of her grandmother, except hers was often more of a breathy "ay-uh" that was more like an inhale than a two-syllable acknowledgment.

"So what's your story? Where are you from?" Lucretia seemed eager to get to know her better.

"Well, I'm an interior designer. Grew up here in Maine. Went to school in New York City. Worked several years there before starting out on my own. I have a studio in Connecticut now. Outside of Hartford."

"Why didn't you say so when we talked this morning? You should help us to redecorate the inn."

"That's certainly a possibility. It could be fun."

"Absolutely. And where did you grow up in Maine?"

"Pennington Point. Just north of Portland."

"Very nice. So beautiful there."

Elizabeth's hand went to a twinge in her gut. "Before last summer, it was. And it was an amazing place to grow up."

"Last summer? . . . Oh, the hurricane."

"Yes." The word was barely audible. She tried to swallow away the tightness in her throat.

"That was quite a storm."

"It was horrible. My family owned and ran an inn there, on the precipice. Had for generations. All that came to an end last summer. The devastation was . . ." As images flashed in the recesses of her mind, Elizabeth felt a gentle hand on her shoulder.

"I'm so sorry."

"Thanks." The pain was surprisingly still raw. "Hard to believe it's been almost a year."

"Will you rebuild?"

Lucretia's question cut to the bone. *What* was *she going to do? Had she come to a decision yet? If she allowed too much time to pass, the decision would be made for her. Had she reached that point yet?*"

"I certainly feel the pressure to rebuild. That was my childhood home. I think my grandmother would want me to."

"Your grandmother?"

"Yeah, she raised me."

Lucretia let it go at that.

Before long they pulled up to a small shop nestled in a string of small businesses. The sign hanging over the door read *International Imports*. It was a quiet side street that didn't appear to be near the water.

"What's this?"

"It's Jonathon's. He has a much bigger place in Portland. I swear he just uses this for storage and doesn't really operate it as a retail outlet. He doesn't have anyone here to greet visitors when he goes on his buying trips. I've actually never set foot in it. I got the sense he really never wanted me to come here. But I'm here now."

The threesome hopped out of her car and approached the front door. The window in the top half was divided into nine panes, all covered on the inside with plain white paper. A peak through the side didn't reveal much.

"So inviting," Elizabeth needled.

"I don't have a key for the place, so this should be interesting." A turn of the knob confirmed it was locked.

Elizabeth fingered the skeleton key concealed in her pocket. It wouldn't have opened it, anyway.

"I guess I'll have to break in."

CHAPTER TWENTY-TWO

"Is there a back d—?"

Lucretia's fist wrapped in the tail of her shirt plowed through the bottom left pane with a crunch, shattering it and sending shards flying. Startled, Elizabeth stepped back while her friend with a battering ram for an arm reached in and turned the knob.

Out of concern for canine paws near the broken glass, Elizabeth returned her pup to the safety of the car and then followed Lucretia as she pushed through the doorway into the small store. Diminutive pieces of furniture were scattered along the front. Stacks of plain tan boxes with small scribbles on the sides took up most of the rest of the tight space. It bore no resemblance to a retail establishment.

"What the hell is he doing here? What *is* all this?" Lucretia grabbed hold of a box and ripped it open. Brushing aside the packing peanuts, she yanked out a large ivory tusk and held it up. "That savage."

"Good God. Did you have any idea this is what he was involved in?"

"Of course not. What do you think?"

"I don't know, Lucretia. I don't really know you *or* Sterling. I have no idea what either one of you is capable of," Elizabeth pushed back.

Tossing the box onto the floor, the innkeeper's wife flopped into one of the spindly chairs that looked like it was too fragile to support even a petite frame like hers. "He's the monster, not me."

"Ya know what, girl? I don't think I care. But I do know I've had my fill." She smacked the nearest stack of boxes. "This weekend was supposed to be a fun getaway, and it's been anything but. In fact, it's been a nightmare that I got wrapped up in and I'm done. I have no desire to get any more involved in this mess."

A deep male voice belted from the back of the store. "Who are you and what the *hell* are you doing here?" A man who looked strikingly like Sterling, perhaps ten to fifteen years older, thundered through the narrow passageway between the boxes.

Lucretia jumped to her feet. "Robert?"

He grinned, apparently recognizing her. "You must be his innocent young bride. Lucy, is it?"

"Lucretia," she corrected.

"Oh, that's right."

"You're his older brother."

"Yeah, I'm sure he doesn't mention us often. He has three older brothers. He was the little runt we didn't let into the family business when our father turned it over to us. A very profitable business, I might add. He was desperate to prove himself, so this was his test." He extended his arm in a flourish as if to show off the stacks. "He was more than willing to take on this responsibility."

Struck by how much he sounded like Jonathon, Elizabeth feared where their encounter was headed.

Lucretia lunged closer. "You convinced him to import illegal ivory? You're an animal."

"An animal? Perhaps. More specifically, a cougar. There's quite a market for this. Certain people will pay big money for ivory. And a sleepy town like this is easy to get shipments in and out of."

"You're disgusting."

"May be. But I'm quite well off. And money has a way of soothing the soul. Something your husband strives for but doesn't seem to be able to grasp."

"Well, he's at the bottom of the harbor, so I don't think that's ever going to happen."

"Is that so?"

"Yeah."

"I guess I should say I'm sorry to hear that."

"Coming from his brother . . . I can't imagine why he would ever look up to you."

"That may be. But he did."

"So very twisted." Lucretia mumbled to herself, "And I thought I loved him."

"Yeah, well, it's hard to know who really deserves to be loved, isn't it?"

A siren approached from the distance. Elizabeth yearned for an out and hoped that was it. As it neared, she inched for the door, but Sterling's brother wasn't having it and pulled a pistol out from behind him, presumably from his waistband.

"You two need to stay put. Not a sound. The local constable has more important matters to worry himself with than this tiny excuse for a shop. Even if there's a knock on the door or a call from beyond, you keep quiet if you know what's good for you." He waved the pistol in the air and then screwed on a silencer.

Blinking away flickering stars in her line of sight, Elizabeth realized her pulmonary function had all but shut down. She took in small gasps of air. Her thoughts went to her pup in the hot car.

Had she remembered to roll down the windows a bit? Visions of him panting with his tongue hanging out to the side made her want to run out the front door in spite of the gun pointed at them.

As the siren grew closer, Sterling's brother fidgeted between the piles with the gun dangling awkwardly in his fingers. The wail reached a crescendo outside the door and then was silenced abruptly.

A car door slammed and footsteps approached, but no knock came. Was the officer at Lucretia's car? She earnestly wanted to take a peek. Was her pup okay? Couldn't he see the broken pane near the knob? Why wasn't he checking out the shop?

Elizabeth couldn't stand it any longer. She lunged for the door, grasping the knob.

The gun-wielding brother yelled for her to stop. A couple shots rang out. The sound of ricocheting made Elizabeth freeze. Behind her, Lucretia slumped to the floor, her body wedged against a small chest.

Outside, Mack ordered everyone inside to put down their weapons and come out the front. Elizabeth dropped to the floor, kneeling next to Lucretia's lifeless body.

"Lucretia, are you all right?" Deep red blood seeped out from underneath her and pooled on the floor. Taking hold of a shoulder, it took everything she had to roll her over onto her back. Pulling her onto her lap, Elizabeth's blood-soaked hand felt strangely warm.

"It's going to be all right. Hang in there," she assured her, hoping her tone didn't reveal her fear.

The chief repeated his orders. Elizabeth glanced toward the rear. No sign of the brother.

"Chief, I think the guy with the gun went out the back," she yelled, desperate to be heard. He didn't acknowledge, but she could hear him on his radio calling for backup. *He'll be long gone before anyone else shows up. Or was he still in the store somewhere?* Lucretia stirred in her arms and groaned.

"Hey, girl, you rest easy. It's going to be all right. Help is on the way." Her words sounded hollow and felt insincere. She stared at Lucretia's eyes, willing them to show signs of life, just a twitch would do, but they remained closed. The entire front of her shirt had turned from a bright white to a deep crimson.

"Chief, call an ambulance!" Lizzi begged.

"This is your last chance. Drop your weapons and come out . . . with your hands where I can see them. *Now!*" Mack bellowed, a hoarseness creeping into his voice. He was alone, and Elizabeth sensed he was not in control of the situation.

Fearful he would start shooting, Elizabeth eased Lucretia off her legs and went to the door, opening it slowly. The chief was crouched next to the cruiser, using the open door as a shield. His weapon was drawn, pointed through the open window, directly at her. She held her hands high above her head and took a few steps. "It's just me and Lucretia Livingston. She's been shot. She needs an ambulance."

Keeping his gun poised with one hand, Mack called for a medical transport on his shoulder mic and then made his way around the door and crept up to Elizabeth. He yanked her by the arm out onto the sidewalk and slipped inside, head darting from side-to-side. On his way through the shop, he regarded Lucretia's bloody body splayed on the floor. Making a full loop, he systematically checked every corner and pushed open the back entrance to check the rear. Clearly, Sterling's brother had taken advantage of the commotion in the front of the store to take his leave out the back and was long gone.

Elizabeth returned to her spot on the floor next to Lucretia and cradled one of her hands in hers, willing against all rational thought for her to be okay. *Where was the ambulance? How long does it take in a small town like this?*

The chief mumbled something into his mic and then made his way back to the front, kneeling next to the two young women. As his hand dropped to Lucretia's neck, Elizabeth was horrified to watch his pudgy fingers search for a pulse. It hadn't crossed her mind that might be necessary. She searched his face, but he remained impassive; his training served him well. A tense silence pervaded the small space until another siren could be heard in the distance. It seemed to have come to a stop somewhere. Nowhere near where it was needed.

"Come on, already!" She laid down the limp hand she'd been holding and started for the doorway, leaning against the jamb.

As the ambulance approached, the undulation echoed in her head. Mack brushed past her, darting out to the parking lot to flag down the EMTs.

Left alone with someone barely clinging to life, lying where she'd dropped after being gunned down, Elizabeth's back stiffened.

Was she still breathing? She couldn't bring herself to check. She feared she already knew the answer.

Lucretia's body took on the appearance of a grotesque theatrical prop—nothing more—left there until the curtain opened again for the opening scene.

The EMTs burst in with the gurney's wheels rattling across the threshold. They abandoned it to drop to the floor and assess the victim's condition. Their neon orange jackets with EMT stamped on the back seemed to brighten the room. Elizabeth hoped it wasn't a false portent. A strong hand pulled her up, leading her outside. She winced as pain awakened near her shoulder and pulled back. Groping at loose fabric hanging from a ragged hole, her fingers explored inside and came out wet.

"What have you got there?" The chief shoved his balding head too close for her liking, and a foul odor of sweat accosted her nose. She leaned away.

"I'm sure it's nothing," she insisted, hoping he would back off and attend to Lucretia, not her.

"Let me see," he insisted and took a firm hold, lifting up her sleeve.

She tried to pull away. "It's fine. I'm—"

"Looks like you got yourself a flesh wound." His eyes traveled to hers as if questioning how she wouldn't have known. "You're one damn lucky lady."

When he finally released her arm, she pulled up her sleeve to see for herself.

"You'll need to get that looked at." As if in response, a third siren could be heard in the distance. "And you are?"

"Elizabeth Pennington. I'm—I'm a friend of Lucretia's." The words sounded odd spilling out of her mouth, yet the chief accepted them without question. She thought for a moment and decided she honestly could say she felt they'd made a connection and would be close friends—that was, if Lucretia survived the cold-blooded shooting.

Neon orange re-emerged through the doorway as an EMT lifted his end of the stretcher over the threshold and negotiated it through the tight space. Lucretia lay neatly tucked under the covers; just her head stuck out. The only blood visible, which stood in sharp disharmony with her fiery red hair, was a swipe on her cheek. The situation suddenly didn't feel so dire. If the EMTs had refrained from covering Lucretia's face so as not to alarm innocent bystanders, Elizabeth appreciated their civility. Could she be okay?

When they slid the gurney into the back, catching the wheels on the rear bumper, Lucretia's head wobbled from side-to-side, jostling long wavy tendrils. Elizabeth worried they'd been too rough with their patient. However, Lucretia appeared undisturbed in her slumber. If only it was as simple as that.

The one-two slam of the rear doors startled Elizabeth. Only then did she notice onlookers scattered throughout the parking lot. A yelp inside Lucretia's car reminded her how patient her pup had been. *The poor thing. What had been going through his mind?* Yanking the door open, she stroked his silky head, relieved to see she had left the window partway open for him.

"You know, he's the reason I showed up here when I did," the chief reprimanded. "Someone called to say a dog had been left in a hot car."

"Really." Taking a hold of Buddy's leash, she stepped back, and he jumped out, wagging his tail and back end. His large pink tongue hung out one side of his mouth.

"Yeah."

"I *did* leave the window open for him," she threw out her feeble defense. Hugging the squirming canine, she stroked his heaving sides, alarmed at the heat radiating off of him.

"Lucky for you the caller either didn't see it or thought that wasn't enough."

The ambulance set off for the hospital with lights flashing and Lucretia secured inside, and the second medical transport pulled up to the same spot. Mack addressed the driver through the open window. She jumped out and dashed to the rear, opening the double doors to retrieve a rectangular orange box.

As Elizabeth's wound was dressed with Buddy sitting nervously at her feet, the small crowd slowly dispersed, chatting amongst themselves as they went. The chief took the opportunity to take Elizabeth's statement, what little she could tell him, before returning her and her furry companion to the inn. *How had she become so intertwined in such a vile mess?*

CHAPTER TWENTY-THREE

So *Sterling's whereabouts* were unknown. He'd managed to escape custody by jumping off the back of a boat. It went without saying authorities were frustrated he'd slipped away and didn't appear to have a clue where he'd ended up. Had he survived the plunge and successfully made his way to shore? Could he still be alive? . . . Lurking in the shadows? Elizabeth prayed it wasn't true. Either way, clearly this was not over if his brother was in town. And if Sterling was hiding out nearby, she could think of a couple places he might be attracted to. She would start with the cellar at the inn.

Rounding the back corner of the old building with her pup at her heels, she groped along a hedge of dense plantings, sorely out of shape and looming over her head, not having felt the sharp edge of a trimmer in a while. Or even a dull edge, for that matter. At about the middle of the wall, Elizabeth could make out the grayed framework of an entrance and thrust her arms in, pulling apart the greenery. The cracked bare wood of the double doors had shed its last chip of paint long ago. They lay at the foot of crumbling stone steps, so besieged with neglect they looked more like a rocky slope than a set of stairs.

"Come on, Bud," she called to her faithful companion, who promptly plopped his back end on the grass.

Elizabeth laughed as she shuffled down the steps, sliding in places where there was no foothold. "Fine, you stay there. Stand guard. Let me know if you see anyone coming."

With no discernable keyhole, it looked as though the doors were locked from the inside. A solitary rusty knob hung at an odd angle. She turned it, giving it a yank, surprised to find the knob in her hand.

"Jesus." Had she broken it? Was it like that to deter people from trying to enter? She would have to find another way in. Examining the entryway more closely, she noticed a primitive latch at the top, across the slit between the two panels. Rotating the latch, she guided it along grooves cut over successive use until it was perpendicular to the ground. She re-inserted the knob and wedged her fingers between the doors, catching an edge. It pulled easily as if used often, though the hinges squeaked in protest.

Propping it open with a loose stone from the steps, she called once more to her pup, "Are you coming?" He slid his front half down into a reclining position and plopped his head on his legs, turned away from her.

"You coward," she grumbled, disappointed she wouldn't have his company in the dark recesses under the inn.

With her first step she was nearly overwhelmed by the mustiness, yet it felt dry. Sunlight from the open doorway did little to penetrate the dark, windowless space. She pulled out her cell and switched on the flashlight. The narrow swath painted a picture of an uneven dirt floor and stone walls along the perimeter of a low ceiling. Large round beams fashioned from tree trunks spanned the width, supporting the weight of the inn. Strands of cobwebs long since abandoned shimmered in her light. Rudimentary wooden shelves lined the wall on one side, which she imagined were used years ago as a sort of root cellar. A large bin that could have held potatoes or parsnips occupied the space next to the shelves. Racks suspended from the ceiling still held what looked to be herb cuttings that had been hung to dry. A sizable pile of dirt in one corner looked like it may have been left over from when the cellar was originally dug.

Her toe caught a chunk of masonry as she crept deeper. She kicked it to the side, careful to step over other pieces as she went. Out on the lawn, Buddy let out a sharp yelp, presumably calling her out of the cellar, not brave enough to accompany her and too impatient to wait quietly.

"Hold on, Bud. I won't be long. Just give me few minutes."

Making her way across the cool cellar floor, her light shined on a set of rickety stairs on the far wall, leading up to the first floor. Where did the door at the top lead? Into the lobby across from Sterling's office? Inside his office? Then it hit her. The cellar only took up half the space under the inn. There had to be another section she couldn't see. The wall on the other side of the stairs looked more recent than the original outer walls and was made of sheetrock panels. Who had blocked it off and why? It was too intriguing not to pursue it.

Starting on the far end and running her fingers all the way around the edges of each panel, she looked for some sort of latch or catch. After she traced the last section without finding anything, she banged on the wall with the side of her hand in frustration. Something clicked, and the panel shifted forward, hinged on the left side.

Pulling it open, she peered into the darkness that seemed to go on forever. She stepped inside, shining her light in a broad sweep of the space.

It was a warehouse of sorts. Next to an old shovel and bucket standing in the corner were cardboard boxes in a variety of shapes and sizes stacked on wooden pallets, presumably to keep them off any moisture that might be in the dirt floor. The stylized modern font on the labels looked incongruous in their antiquated surroundings. Elizabeth approached the boxes, running her fingers across the top of them. Very little dust. They'd been placed there recently.

The voice behind her was so close, she could almost feel hot breath on her neck.

"What are you looking for?"

She whirled around and flashed her light in Ben's face. He swatted at it without making contact so she adjusted the tilt, taking a broader aim at his torso. He held a lantern at his side, which he lifted and cranked the wick higher, brightening the cellar and bleaching the walls with its glare. Not willing to give up her source of illumination, she held onto her cell, even though it was lost in the lantern's light.

"What are you doing here? Do you know anything about this?" She nodded toward her find.

"You might want to be minding your business around here. Saw your dog outside the door and knew you were snooping. Shouldn't you be heading out of town? The wedding you came for is not going to happen. You've got no reason to stay."

Elizabeth ignored his rude invitation to leave. "Someone has stashed this here. Do you know when that wall was built? Or who built it? It looks fairly new."

He remained tight-lipped. She noticed a camera bag rested on one hip, its wide strap hung from the opposite shoulder, crossing his chest. A pair of Ls engraved on the flap shined in the fleeting light. He pushed it around to his backside.

"I'm sure you're aware things aren't what they seem around here," Elizabeth pressed.

"Like I said, get on out. You shouldn't be down here. It's off-limits to guests."

"What are *you* doing here? What is your connection with the inn? And this family?"

"Girl, leave well enough alone." He held firm, not willing to disclose if he had intimate knowledge.

She needed to push further. "What is it between you and Lucretia?"

His eyes narrowed. "Between us?"

"Are you lovers?" Not that she would blame Lucretia. The cowboy might have had her by ten years or so, but there was something enticing about him. God, she loved his slow Western drawl.

"Careful."

"Did Sterling find out?"

"I *said* . . . careful." He remained calm, not allowing her to provoke him.

"Well, you should know that she just got rushed to the hospital."

His eyes flashed. "Lucretia?"

"Yeah, we were over at Sterling's store in East Boothbay and his brother showed up with a gun."

"His brother? Didn't know he had any brothers."

"Yeah, guess he has three. This one was Robert."

"And he shot Lucretia?" Taking a step closer, his eyes took on an urgency she hadn't seen before.

"Yeah. She was rushed to the hospital. Probably in surgery right now." Elizabeth didn't intend to give him false hope, but she also didn't want to be the bearer of such grave news. Someone else would have to shoulder that responsibility. Someone who got paid to do it.

As he fled, the glowing lantern caught on the panel opening, knocking it from his hand, shattering the glass panels on the dirt floor. Leaving it where it lay, he dashed across the cellar, heading for the light from the open doorway, slipping once on uneven ground. He disappeared, shoving aside the old wooden panel that swung back to half open.

Re-sealing the secret storage area, Elizabeth stamped out the flickering flame, foot crunching on the glass shards, and headed back across the dirt floor. The police would have to figure out what her discovery was all about.

Overwhelmed by the chaos and tragedy at the inn, Elizabeth dropped off the skeleton key at the front desk, relieved to give up possession of it, and strode to her car parked in the far corner of the lot, bathed in the blissful shade of a mature evergreen. Having packed it earlier, all that stood between them and their trip home was a stop at a gas station on the way out of town. Chief McKenzie knew how to reach her if he needed to. And he had promised to give her an update on Lucretia once he'd heard something.

Before they reached her car, Elizabeth stopped short, so her pup hesitated, looking to her for direction. A small tote sat on the ground near the left back tire. She recognized it as her emergency kit she kept in her trunk and, by the grace of God, had never had to pull out before. Inching closer she scooped up the bag and noticed a puddle of something dark next to it beneath the trunk. Had it been there when she pulled in? Was something leaking from her car? She scanned the area for anything else that looked aberrant. Releasing the latch on the trunk and lifting the lid, she froze. A short puff of air was all she was able to manage. Taking a step backward, she dropped the tote on her foot.

"Ana!"

CHAPTER TWENTY-FOUR

A *sharp pain jabbed* between her eyes. Her stomach wasn't in much better shape. At the sight of the body in her trunk, nestled between the spare and reusable grocery totes, Elizabeth had nearly retched her last meal. She ambled over to the grass and flopped down. Nausea continued to roll through her abdomen, not showing any indication of settling down any time soon. Drawn to the smell, her pup had to be coaxed into following her and lying patiently on the grass alongside. He nudged his moist nose into her gut as if he knew where one of the issues was. Between her head and her stomach, she had all the makings of a miserable hangover without the satisfaction of having a grand time the night before. Stroking the silky warm fur on his haunches, she prayed the atrocity in her trunk wouldn't somehow pull her into the investigation. Surely the police would realize she had nothing to do with it. . . . *Wouldn't they?*

In retrospect, her rationale for dropping everything and dashing off to Maine to attend the wedding of a high school acquaintance—one she couldn't recall having more than a casual conversation with—completely escaped her. *What had she been thinking?* Sure, she'd been working hard for months on end to build her studio and could use a break. But a long weekend hundreds of miles away was turning out to be one of her less-than-brilliant ideas—although not as utterly stupid as walking away from a potential relationship with an amazing guy last summer.

Just being near him made her feel tingly all over, even more than when the star quarterback opened his locker that was right next to hers, senior year of high school. In spite of Lucretia's urging, even if she could track him down, she couldn't very well go crawling back to him in the hopes he felt the same way about her. *What if he didn't?* He certainly hadn't chased after her. Elizabeth couldn't bear the thought of his rejection. Suddenly she felt achingly alone in spite of her furry pal at her side.

The police car arrived with lights flashing and siren wailing. The closer he got, the more Elizabeth's head threatened to split open. "Bud, I want this nightmare over with so we can go home," she lamented. Drawing him closer to her, she planted a kiss on the top of his head. His sweet brown eyes searched hers for a clue to what was going on.

Pulling herself to her feet, her knees started to buckle. She lunged onto the hood of her car, breathing deep to allow her head to clear. Mack was already out of his cruiser and rounding the front when his eyes went to her trunk with the lid partially raised. He shuffled toward the scene with arms dangling awkwardly at his sides, chest puffed out as if trying to convince himself of his bravery. With an upturned index finger, he flicked the lid open. For a seasoned lawman, his suddenly ashen face seemed uncharacteristic.

"What happened?" His voice was low and raspy. She imagined he'd had to ask the question far too many times lately.

"Like I told you on the phone, I was trying to head out and found this—" She wasn't quite sure what to call her find and didn't want to be disrespectful but needed to distance herself from any connection with the deceased. "I opened my trunk and there she was."

He leaned in, examining the contents, and then stepped back. "Oh God, it's Ana." His shoulders slumped and his fingers slid through the thinning gray hair on one side of his head. Turning his focus to the unfortunate, unsuspecting owner of the car, he asked, "Did you know her?"

Elizabeth felt herself backpedaling. She couldn't get pulled into any kind of police investigation. "Not really. I met her in Chauncey's on Saturday. She was waiting tables when I stopped in there."

"When was the last time you saw her?"

She imagined these were the first two questions on his standard list he asked every suspect.

"Let's see. I guess it was yesterday afternoon." So much had happened since then, it seemed as though their encounter in the loft was days ago.

"The afternoon? What time?"

"Time? Oh, I'd say it was around four o'clock."

"Where?"

Where? She wasn't going to confess to snooping around where guests didn't usually go. "In the carriage house. I was admiring the old building and she happened by."

"Any idea why she was here?"

"No, but I wouldn't think it was unusual for her to be here. From what I understand, she and Lucretia are quite close. Like sisters. Grew up together."

"True," he acknowledged and stepped farther back to survey the area around her car. "What's with the bag on the pavement? Is that yours?"

"Yeah, it's mine. That's actually the reason I opened my trunk. I'd packed everything into the car earlier, but when we walked up a little while ago, I noticed the bag. I almost missed it since it was partially under the back end."

"But you remembered putting it in?"

"I never took it out. It's my bag of emergency supplies if my car breaks down. Jumper cables, flares. I put our stuff behind the front seats. Never opened the trunk. . . . If I hadn't noticed it, I would have driven off and taken the body with me back to Connecticut." Her stomach turned over and a new wave of nausea rolled in.

"Well, whoever dumped the body was hoping that's exactly what you'd do."

Whoever? Was she clear of any implication she had something to do with this?

"Of course, you're not going anywhere now."

Ugh! All she wanted was to clear out of there and leave the inn far behind. Now she was trapped. . . . Or was it just her car that was being detained against its will?

"Look, Chief, I really need to get back to Connecticut. I've got a business to run, clients who are expecting to meet with me, deadlines looming." Her words rung a bit odd to her ears with respect to the grave situation they were dealing with; they were a slight exaggeration, but she needed to make a point.

"Well, maybe you could rent a car and leave yours here for us to process. It could take some time."

"Rent a car? I can't afford that." Was he serious? "Besides, I don't leave my car in anyone else's hands. I don't let anyone else drive it. This is my baby. I worked hard to afford this—"

"All right, all right," he grumbled. "This isn't something that happens quickly. It's a process that takes time. . . . I'll see what I can do." He stepped away and pulled out his cell, presumably conferring with the team working on forensics at the antiques shop.

Elizabeth's thoughts returned to the body. She was grateful she hadn't gotten to know Ana very well. Who could have done this to her? With Sterling out of the picture, she thought of Ben. They knew each other from the bar, and they didn't seem to get along well. Was there more to it than that? What motive would he have? Did he know about Ana's relationship with Lucretia? If he was romantically linked with Lucretia, how far would a cowboy from Montana go to eliminate competition? She shuddered to think she was alone with him in the cellar earlier.

Out of the corner of her eye, she caught movement—someone walking toward the front of the inn. The not-to-be bride. Elizabeth felt an obligation to approach her, offer words of regret, sorrow. She wasn't sure what she was going to say, exactly. But she needed to offer some sort of condolences. Was her fiancé still missing, presumed dead? Thought to be alive? Judging from the rhythmic sound of shovels through the closed doors of the carriage house, the ground-penetrating radar equipment must have given them reason to dig, but she doubted it was public knowledge what they were doing and who they were looking for.

"Natalia!" Lizzi called to her. Assuring the chief she'd be right back, she dashed toward the walkway. Once she grew close enough, Elizabeth reached out to touch her arm and spoke softly.

"Elizabeth . . . I didn't know you had come."

Regretting her thoughtlessness for not responding properly to the wedding invitation, she offered, "I'm so sorry I wasn't able to let you know sooner—so many things were up in the air—but at the last minute I was able to get away. I really wanted to be here."

Edward's fiancée remained silent, as if she hadn't heard Elizabeth's words.

"Natalia, I'm so sorry to hear about Edward. How awful."

The awkward, high school acquaintance dropped her eyes to the pavement. "Thank you." Her voice wobbled with her words.

"Is there any news yet?" Elizabeth didn't dare ask anything more specific than that.

"No. All I can think is the worst. Something terrible has happened. I can feel it. "

"You haven't seen him since Wednesday?"

218

"For me, it was Tuesday night. We got together for dinner, but that was going to be the last time we saw each other before the ceremony. My family's customs are very strict about that. We were to see each other again on Saturday afternoon when I walked down the aisle."

"There was no rehearsal the evening before?"

"No. The wedding was so small, it really wasn't necessary. And with a rehearsal, there needs to be a rehearsal dinner, and we really couldn't afford that. . . . Now I wish we'd had plans for something the night before or Thursday night. We would have known something was wrong much sooner."

"How long had he worked at the inn?" Elizabeth steered the conversation away from the inevitable downward spiral.

Her face brightened as she gathered her thoughts. "Oh, he was one of the first hires when the inn opened. He was so excited about working here. He and Lucretia seemed to click."

"They seemed to 'click'?"

"Yeah." Natalia's eyes narrowed as if offended by Elizabeth's question. "I don't mean anything other than they got along well, and he was able to make suggestions, contribute to running the inn."

"That's great. It certainly makes it less like a job and more like a passion when you get along well with your boss."

"Yes, it does. He really enjoyed it. He was so proud to be a part of the inn. He even went along with Lucretia's idea to use old-fashioned bellhop uniforms. He looked so cute in his." Elizabeth thought back to her first night there and the bellhop who stopped to help when she was fumbling with her key to the room. "They were so adorable. And unique. The guests loved them. I think they brought the inn back in time, where it should be."

"Were the others on board with the idea?"

"Well, yes. That is, until Mr. Sterling arrived. He didn't want anything to do with it. He made it quite clear he didn't approve of the idea. He wanted the staff uniforms to be more updated . . . and more casual. If you ask me, that didn't really blend with the elegant décor of the inn. Poor Mrs. Sterling. She had to take a back seat and let her husband run the inn as he wanted to." Her head drooped and her glance shifted to the side. "I know when Edward and I get married, it will be a fifty/fifty proposition. He'd never dominate me like Mr. Sterling does. No way. He's too sweet and caring."

Out of respect, Elizabeth allowed time for her to dwell on her last thought and then asked, "Do the police have any leads as to what happened to your fiancé . . . Edward?"

"I haven't heard of anything yet." She snorted in an unladylike way. "I think they suspect he got cold feet. But I know better. He and I love each other. Very much. I may not have ever been the prom queen, but Edward thinks I'm beautiful."

Feeling a twinge in her gut, Elizabeth revisited faded images from the night of her junior prom.

"I'm sure he does. Why wouldn't he? You're such a sweet person, and you look amazing. I almost didn't recognize you."

"Elizabeth, that's more than kind of you." Her face found new color, and she averted her eyes. "You were always kind to me in high school. Unlike most others." Her voice trailed off.

Elizabeth laid a hand on Natalie's forearm. "I'm so sorry for what you're having to go through. I'll say a prayer that they'll find him safe and sound." She hoped her expression didn't imply she suspected a different outcome.

"I try not to think otherwise. But if something did happen to my Edward, I bet that bartender had something to do with it. Or at least he knows something about it."

"Do you mean Ben . . . from Chauncey's?"

"Yeah."

"What makes you say that?"

"I don't know. He always seems to be around the inn. Every time I stop by, he's here. But why? He doesn't work here. He has no business here. It's like he's snooping. Edward seemed to be friendly with him, but I just don't trust him."

"Did you tell that to the police?"

"Of course."

"Any idea why he'd be here? Do you think he's looking for something?"

Pausing to consider the question, Natalia tilted her head and shrugged one shoulder up to it in a halfhearted effort.

Hesitating at first, Elizabeth felt compelled to ask, "Do you think he and Lucretia . . . could be involved?"

Countering her puzzled expression, Elizabeth made it clearer. "Lovers."

Wide eyes were followed by a petite hand pressed to her lips. Apparently that thought hadn't crossed her mind. Elizabeth let it drop, repulsed at herself for desecrating Lucretia's image.

After an awkward hug and an exchange of well wishes, Elizabeth returned to her car and the shell-shocked chief.

Hours later, with the sun long past set, the dead body had been removed, every inch of the car dusted for fingerprints, and all traces of bodily fluids removed from the trunk. She'd been given the okay to proceed on her way. She couldn't get behind the wheel fast enough, shaking off her gruesome discovery.

Figuring she'd allowed enough time for Rashelle to catch up on her sleep, she tried her cell one more time. After a couple rings, her friend picked up.

"Yeah." Her tone was gruff with the breeze blowing in the background.

"Hey, Shelle! You're awake."

"Unfortunately, yeah . . . gotta go . . . to work."

"You have to go back to *work*? After spending the weekend there?"

"Yeah, 'course I do. It wasn't like I was actually working all weekend. I was supposed to be there this morning. But they let me get some rest."

"Well, I'm heading back to Connecticut. Was hoping to swing by and say hello on my way out of town. . . . Ya know, get one of your famous Shelle hugs." Elizabeth grinned, remembering how great it felt to be in Rashelle's arms.

"Ha! Well, don't know if I can make that happen. As usual, I'm late. I'm walking to my car now. . . . Where the *hell* did I park the damn thing?"

Elizabeth considered making her case for stopping by the inn where Rashelle worked but felt a brush-off coming on. It seemed a bit late in the day to be heading into work, even at an inn. Having grown up in one, she was familiar with the ins and outs of the hospitality industry. Then it hit her. Rashelle wasn't rushing off to work. She was off to see a guy. It was always a guy. She was lying to her again. For her, it was always about drinking and guys. She hadn't changed at all since college.

"Oh, there it is. Boy, I must have really been out of it. Don't remember leaving it there. Oh, *shit*! I've got a ticket. What the f—? Oh, stupid me. I parked in front of a fire hydrant. *Damn it!* I can't afford that. How much is that going to cost me? Look, Lizzi, I gotta go. I'll catch up with you at some point. I'm sorry. I'll see ya."

With the click in her ear, Elizabeth realized she'd spent the last several years working much harder at their friendship than Rashelle ever had. It had always been one-sided. Elizabeth had been there for her whenever she needed her, time and time again; but at the moment Rashelle couldn't make the time for her, even though it had been months since they'd seen each other. And now it was time for Elizabeth to let go. It hurt, but she acknowledged the hurt may have been more a matter of her kicking herself for allowing Rashelle to drag her along all those years, thinking she was her friend. The emptiness taking up space in her gut was all too familiar, and she tried to push it aside. Reaching over to stroke the warm fur of her canine friend, she thanked God for his unconditional love. Yet, her heart ached for something more.

CHAPTER TWENTY-FIVE

L eaving the inn behind, too tired to care about anything except getting back on the road to Connecticut, Elizabeth tossed her cell into the console. She never thought she would feel this way, but there was no reason to stay in Maine any longer. Apparently the only one she could depend upon was her canine pal in the passenger seat. Buddy was so forgiving and flexible. He was just happy to be with her. Lord, she wished she could run across a guy who felt the same way. Having a pup had relieved some of the emptiness, but there had to be more to a fulfilling existence. She was sure of it. She counted on it.

Her headlights cut a swath in the fog rolling in from the harbor. Having to wait for her car to be cleared by the authorities, it was much later than she'd hoped to head out. But she had no intention of staying another night at the inn. There were too many reasons not to; Topping the list were Ana's killer on the loose, as well as the uncertainty surrounding Sterling's whereabouts. His body hadn't been recovered yet, although that seemed imminent. Her heart went out to Lucretia. She prayed she'd made it through surgery and was going to recover. Lingering bloody images pushed their way back to the forefront of her mind. She'd never seen so much blood before. Her gut felt as though someone had given it a good swift kick. Why Lucretia? She was someone Elizabeth could connect with. And not someone who deserved the tortuous hand she'd been dealt.

There was also Sterling's brother, Robert, who had disappeared out the back of the antique store, eluding police who were focused on tending to a gunshot victim. Where had he made off to? If Lucretia did make it through surgery, was she still in danger?

Elizabeth reluctantly pulled the car to the side of the road and shoved the gearshift into neutral, keeping a firm foot on the brake. Buddy lifted his head as if to question why they suddenly stopped. She reached over and stroked his soft warm head.

"I know, Bud. I'm having second thoughts. I don't think we can leave just yet. I want to go home as much as you do, but Lucretia may still need our help. This isn't over." She listened to the purr of the engine and watched the fog drift unevenly through her headlight beams. If she sat there long enough, it would lull her to sleep, and she didn't have time for that. Her head was telling her to put it back into first and get the hell out of there, but her instincts were telling her she was the only one who knew all the pieces of what was going on. *Get back in the game.* Could anyone else identify Robert? And if the innkeeper's wife had survived, she could use a friend right now. Unbeknownst to Lucretia, her best friend was just fished out of a trunk. Elizabeth's trunk. Would she look guilty by leaving town? . . . Or by returning to the scene of the crime?

No matter. Either way, she couldn't leave without making sure Lucretia was going to be all right. Who else would be concerned about her? And she also needed to make sure the Sterling brothers were out of the picture. And what about the cowboy from Montana? What was his story? There was more to find out.

Jamming the stick into first, she grabbed the left side of the wheel and cut a hard left, making a U-turn across the road, kicking up gravel as she caught the shoulder with her back tire. Buddy sat up, shifting his paws to brace himself in the turn.

"It's okay, Bud. Lie down." He remained upright, struggling not to sail off the seat.

As she hit the gas, something slipped from the bushes along the side of the road into the beams of her headlights. Elizabeth tapped the brakes and squinted to discern the form paused on the center line. It was white. Billowy. Like a woman in a long nightgown, undulating in the evening breeze. She was gazing in the opposite direction, toward the inn, as if she didn't notice the idling car behind her.

Elizabeth stepped out, leaving the door ajar. Buddy slipped out behind her and let out a low growl. "Stay, Bud," she ordered, slipping a finger through his collar while keeping an eye on the ethereal figure. "Hello?" The woman didn't seem to hear. "Lucretia?" She turned her upper body as a billow of fog rolled in between them. Elizabeth crept closer. "Is that you?" She peered into the swirling white but could no longer see the figure.

Time felt suspended as she held fast, hoping to catch a glimpse of her again. *What had just happened?* She was afraid to accept what she'd seen.

A vehicle approaching from behind snapped her back to the reality she was standing in the middle of an active road. Ushering her pup into the car, she scrambled in behind him and resumed their trek toward the inn, feeling like she was returning to the enemy's lair. As she neared the entrance the vehicle behind her drew closer. Elizabeth squinted her eyes at the high beams in her rearview mirror. They followed her into the parking lot. As she pulled into the first open slot, a pickup truck stopped behind her, blocking her way out. She climbed out with a hand on her pup's collar. He might not have been a ferocious guard dog, but he was loyal to her. It was better than confronting someone alone.

She saw the silhouette of his cowboy hat as he rounded the front of the truck.

"Thought you would have been long gone by now," he grumbled.

"Yeah, me too. But then I realized someone needed to be here who's on Lucretia's side."

"What, you don't think I am?"

"Ben, I have no idea. All I know is Lucretia can't speak for herself right now."

His eyes fell to the tips of his boots. "No, she can't."

"Did you go to the hospital?"

"Yeah." He didn't look up.

It pained Elizabeth to ask, but she had to know. "What's going on?"

He stepped back and leaned against the front quarter panel as if he needed the support. "I don't know. I couldn't stand the waiting around. Not knowing. She was still in surgery when I left. Seemed like she'd been there for hours. I just couldn't stand it anymore. I left." Clearly feeling he'd abandoned her, he removed his hat before mussing his hair and slapped the Stetson back on.

Elizabeth stepped in. "It's hard to hang out in a hospital like that. I'm sure she's in good hands." The ghostly image from the road reappeared in her mind, and she pushed it away.

"Hope you're right." He kicked the toe of one boot with the other and jingled the keys in his pocket. "I gotta go. Things to take care of."

Elizabeth remained near her car while Ben pulled the truck to the far end of the lot where there were plenty of open spaces. She watched as he crossed the lawn and disappeared behind the inn. Unable to resist, she set out to see what he was up to. As she rounded the back corner, he headed up the steps to the old cemetery. *Could he be the grave robber?*

Dashing across the backyard with Buddy right behind her, she paused at the crumbling steps and turned to her pup. "Bud, stay," she whispered. She pressed her palm toward his nose to emphasize her command, hoping he'd mind, and then slipped through the overgrown pines. When she reached the fringes of the burial grounds and peered through the boughs, she could see him, shovel in hand. He had a small portable light of some sort set on the stone wall that encircled the space.

Creeping across the uneven ground, she struggled to navigate with limited ambient light. Her toe whacked something hard, and she caught herself from tumbling headfirst over a tombstone. Elizabeth's fingers found the curved edge of the top of it. The cold from the stone penetrated her hands.

"Who's there?"

She no longer had the element of surprise in her favor.

"It's me, Ben." Before she could utter anything else, he had the light directed in her face. Throwing a hand up to block the glare, she stepped clear of the stone that had tripped her up.

Buddy let out a yelp as he brushed past her. Lunging to grab onto his collar, her feet slipped out from underneath her, sending her sprawling in the tall grass. She scrambled to get upright, struggling to hold onto the pup's collar.

"What are you doing?" Her eyes went from the shovel in his grasp to the pile of dirt to the hole it had come out of. "You did this?" Elizabeth was at a loss. "How could you?"

"How could I?"

Buddy let out a low growl, and she shushed him.

"Ben, this is a serious crime. What do you think you're accomplishing by doing this?"

"It's not what you think. I've got to make things right."

"What, do you have . . . a score to settle?"

"That, I do, but this is not—"

"What's that all about?"

"Don't get me started."

"Tell me. Who are you angry at?" Could there be anything to the rumors he killed the Livingstons?

"I'm not really angry at anyone. Life itself, I guess. It's been so damn hard."

CHAPTER TWENTY-FIVE

"What was it like?"

"There you go again, sticking your nose where it shouldn't be. . . . I'm sure you wouldn't understand."

"Try me," she pressed.

He hesitated before poking the shovel into the pile next to him. His hands found his hips.

"My mom was a single parent. Worked so hard and did the best she could. I never knew my father, but I learned to hate him, wherever he was."

Elizabeth considered his story. "At least you had one parent."

"You don't know what it was like," he snapped. "It was hell. Especially after my grandparents passed away, leaving us completely on our own. And then she got into a terrible car accident that left her unable to work and addicted to pain meds. We lost our house. I bet you have no idea what it's like to live in a shelter."

"Can't say that I do. Sorry to hear. But how is this payback?" She gestured to his handiwork.

"It's not." He smacked a hand against the handle of the shovel.

"Is that why you came all the way out here? To get even with your lot in life?"

"No. You're missing the point."

"Maybe she is. But you don't have a right to take matters into your own hands." Chief McKenzie appeared from behind the line of trees along the cemetery. "I'm afraid you're going to have to come with me. We don't tolerate grave robbing, no matter how unfair you think your life has been."

"It's not what it looks like," Ben implored. "You've got the wrong idea."

"No, son. You're the one with the wrong idea."

With head hung low, Ben allowed the chief to snap on the cuffs and take him into custody without resisting. Saddened by the bartender's deplorable actions, Elizabeth followed behind the twosome as they headed out front to the waiting cruiser in the parking lot. Unconcerned with the incident, Buddy found interesting places to nudge his nose along the way.

After securing the prisoner into his back seat, Mack called to her. "Miss Pennington, why are you sticking around?"

"I guess I feel the need to stay for Lucretia."

He sauntered over and lowered his voice. "That's one of the kindest gestures I've witnessed in a long time. You're a good person, Elizabeth. Your instincts are honorable. Don't you worry. I'm looking out for Lucretia. So is the rest of this town. She's been through hell and back, but she still has her hometown for support. You go ahead and hit the road. I'll let you know how things turn out. The best thing you can do right now is to keep her in your prayers . . . and you can do that from anywhere."

She laughed in guarded frivolity. "Thanks, Chief. I appreciate that. I really should get back."

"Of course you should. I know your weekend here didn't turn out like you planned."

"Please stay on Sterling's brother's trail. He's dangerous. He looks just like Jonathon, just a bit older."

"Will do. You can count on that. Now go. Get back to your life."

Elizabeth wondered what would become of the inn and the property if Lucretia wasn't around to care for it. She envisioned waist-high grass obstructing the view of the circular drive, vines covering cracked pillars, and boarded-up windows, dredging up painful memories of the summer before. Her family's inn stood in limbo, waiting for the only person who could change its predicament to make the decision to do so. She considered the condition it must be in after sitting neglected for so long. *What was she waiting for? What was she afraid of?*

As the patrol car pulled away, she called to her pup. He scampered toward her and bounded onto the passenger seat. Relieved to have been released from her self-imposed commitment to Lucretia, she made her way around to the other side and slipped between her car and a white nondescript commercial van parked next it. Behind her was the sound of the door sliding open. A clammy hand clamped onto her mouth and pulled her inside. The last thing she heard was Sterling's voice.

"You should have left town when you had the chance."

CHAPTER TWENTY-SIX

A throbbing *between her* eyes woke Elizabeth in an unfamiliar place. The top of her head was wedged against a hard surface. She was lying on her side. Something pressed against her mouth. She couldn't open her lips. Her shoulders ached from what felt like someone holding her arms behind her. A sour smell crept into her nose, filling her nasal cavities.

Shouting close by startled her. The darkness was pierced by a light bouncing around the tight space. Fuzziness pervaded. There was scuffling. A fist or an elbow jabbed into her thigh. A muffled grunt was all she could muster. She tried to tuck in her legs, but her body lurched with her efforts. Something was tight around her ankles.

A dog barked off in the distance. It sounded agitated. Or at least concerned. The incessant barking grew familiar. Where had

she left her pup? Where was she? Who were the men? Then came
a voice that might prove to be on her side.

"Get out of there, you scum. Stand up on your own two feet.
Hold still. Hands behind your back. Officer, cuff him."

As she could make out more of her surroundings, she wriggled
herself into a sitting position. Pain stabbed the back of her head
and ran down her neck. Her body shook with a sudden chill. She
was inside a van of some sort with only the driver and passenger
seats up front. Half a dozen small cardboard boxes were stacked up
on one side. Rope was coiled in a back corner, and a small duffle
sat on top of the console between the seats. As she dropped her
legs out the sliding door opening, she realized she was looking
at her own car. Buddy was frantic in the driver's seat, clawing at
the window, barking to sound the alert Elizabeth was in danger.
She yearned to reach out and hug him, assure him she was okay,
feel his warm soft fur against her cheek. But she was powerless,
bound at the wrists and ankles, struggling to sit without toppling
over the edge of the open doorway.

"Miss, are you all right?" Before the officer allowed her to
answer, he informed her there was an ambulance on the way and
pulled a Swiss Army knife from his pocket. Elizabeth jumped as
he flipped open the blade a bit closer to her face than she cared
for. He leaned down and slit the duct tape, releasing her ankles.
Turning away slightly, she offered him her bound hands, and he
ran the blade across the tape twice before her arms sprung back
around to her front. Rubbing her wrists and ankles, she endeavored
to restore the circulation. He reached up to free her mouth, but
she threw an arm up to intercept him.

"Mmph!"

He stopped short of his target and shrunk back. She turned away from his reach and found a corner of the tape. Holding her breath she closed her eyes and pulled, certain she'd removed a layer of skin along with it.

"Damn that hurts!" Running a palm across her lower face, she expected to see blood.

The officer's shoulder mic squawked, and he turned his attention to it. Grabbing it with one hand, he cocked his head to the side. "Base, this is Jenkins at the Livingston estate. What's the ETA on the ambulance?"

Wincing from her tactile examination of the raised area on the back of her skull, Elizabeth insisted, "Oh, that won't be necessary. I'm fine. Really."

"We'll let the EMTs give you a once-over to be sure."

Elizabeth leaned out and peered around to the end of the van where the cruiser was parked with its lights flashing. Turning away from the glare, she thought she saw Sterling's profile as Jenkins' partner guided him into the back seat. "Was that Sterling?"

"Yes, ma'am."

"That's who grabbed me?"

"Yes."

"That lucky son of a bitch. Can't believe he's still alive." She blinked to try to clear the throbbing. "My head is *killing* me. What did he hit me with—a crowbar?"

"It's hard to say exactly what it was."

"How the hell did you find me?"

"We've been on the lookout for an unmarked white commercial van ever since the shooting this afternoon. Eyewitnesses reported seeing one leaving the area about that time. We've been looking all over, even extended the search to the train stations and airports, but it was right here."

"Good god."

"Yeah, I don't think he was planning on hanging around much longer. We got here just in time."

Elizabeth shuddered to think what he'd planned to do with her. Struggling to conceive how he could have survived his jump off the back of a boat, she was relieved he was finally in custody. Sliding gingerly out of the confined space, she grabbed the door-jamb to steady herself as her wobbly feet landed on the pavement. She needed to get to Buddy, release him from the confines of the car, and assure him she was okay. Her head spun with her first step, so she lunged for the side mirror.

"Easy, miss."

"I'm fine. Really."

She shook off his firm hand on her upper arm. Yanking the handle, she freed her pup who bounded out of the car with his back end wiggling, nearly sprawling onto the pavement. She let go of the door, and it swung back to rest, slightly ajar. Buddy whimpered at her feet, staying low to the ground, appearing weary of jumping up on her.

"Bud, it's okay. I'm okay." She struggled to stroke his back, missing her mark as he squirmed. "Bud, settle down. It's okay." A glistening on the pavement told her he'd lost control and urinated from all the excitement. He suddenly became still and dropped his head. She could see the whites of his eyes. He knew he'd done something wrong. "Oh, Bud, you poor thing."

She hugged him as tight as she dared and then led him over onto the grass where they sat, her arms around his heaving body. His fur reeked of a sour, nervous sweat he'd never produced before, at least not since she'd adopted him. "It's okay." He rested his head on her shoulder.

As the siren of the third ambulance of the day grew louder, the squad car with Sterling inside pulled away. Elizabeth allowed herself to feel cautious relief at the sight but prayed he wouldn't escape custody again. He'd turned out to be a slimy Brit.

Her pup allowed the EMTs to examine Elizabeth's injuries but sat close by, watching their every move. The two twenty-somethings kept a wary eye on him in case he got too protective. She was thankful they weren't the same medics who showed up earlier at the antique store. Must have been a different shift. They eyed the fresh bandage on her arm and, thankfully, didn't ask.

Another emergency vehicle approached with siren blaring and flashing lights. An ambulance? Seemed excessive. Probably a slow night. Turned out to be a squad car. The chief clambered out, stopping to check in with Jenkins who had remained behind, and strutted over to where Elizabeth sat cross-legged on the grass, having the gash on the back of her head addressed.

"Miss Pennington, I thought you were halfway back to the Nutmeg State by now. You do seem to have gotten yourself tangled up in all the shit that's going on around here." He rested his pudgy hands on his hips, arching his back to establish his presence at the scene.

"Yeah, that was my plan all along." Seriously, Mack? Back off. She wasn't interested in his attempt at humor. With her head splitting, she was in no mood for his prodding. Having had her fill of the twisted happenings in the deceptively sleepy harbor town, she wanted out of there. As her grandmother would have said, it would be a cold day in hell before she ever returned.

Once the EMTs wrapped up and concluded she didn't need transporting, she bid farewell to Mack and his officers. He assured her he'd be in touch with more questions. She acknowledged the probability.

After gulping down a half dozen ibuprofen with warm, no-longer-sparkling water from a half-full bottle sitting in her cup holder, she sped down the circular drive with the inn and its wretched goings-on in the rearview mirror, steadily receding behind her. It was the best thing she'd seen since she'd arrived a few days earlier. She couldn't get down the harbor road fast enough.

Stroking the warm, gentle curve of her pup's soft head, a wave of relief coursed through her. "We're really leaving this time, Bud." As her thoughts drifted to Lucretia in the hospital, Elizabeth fought to remain positive against what seemed to be insurmountable odds. Her free hand drifted to the bandage on her arm. She flinched as her fingers caught the edges of the tape.

There was a tug in her gut that came from running away. The sad and horrific acts she'd witnessed couldn't be erased from her memory. She'd also lost a friend—or rather, she discovered someone she thought was her friend all these years really wasn't. She'd been played the fool. More importantly, she may have lost someone who she sincerely believed she could be real friends with. She prayed Lucretia would pull through.

While taking comfort in the fact Sterling was finally in custody, she was sickened at the havoc he'd wreaked in the short time he was at the helm of the inn and married to Lucretia. The greater the distance between Elizabeth and the Livingston estate, the better. Turning onto Route 27 felt as though she'd finally escaped a giant spider's sticky web. She kept her eyes forward with one hand on her pup's back, oblivious to the danger left behind, curled up on the seat and snoring in contented slumber.

A ringing in the console made her release her foot from the gas and pull off to the side onto a narrow breakdown lane. Buddy jolted awake and sat up straight on his haunches, looking for the reason they'd stopped. Retrieving her phone, she didn't recognize the number, but it was a Maine area code.

"Elizabeth Pennington."

"Miss Pennington, Chief McKenzie."

Please, Lord, let it be good news.

"Yes, Chief? Please don't ask me to come back. I'm already out of town, and I really need to—"

"Miss Pennington, I thought you would want to know. . . . It looks like Miss Livingston is going to make it. She was in ICU for a while after surgery, but they just moved her out of that unit a little while ago."

"Oh, that's wonderful news. So surgery went well?"

"Yeah, well, apparently they lost her at one point, but they were able to revive her."

Elizabeth recalled the ethereal image on the harbor road earlier. "Oh, Lord."

"Yeah, pretty scary. . . . She'll need some time to recover, but it looks like the worst is behind her."

"Thanks for calling to tell me. What a relief. So good to hear."

"I think the whole town shares your relief. Everyone was pulling for her. Fortunately she's a strong lady. She's been through quite a lot in her short life . . . and if anyone was going to survive in her situation, it was her."

As Elizabeth tucked her phone back into the console, she brushed an unexpected tear from the corner of her eye before it could trickle down her cheek.

CHAPTER TWENTY-SEVEN

The night sky was as dark as the deep water in the harbor she'd left behind, and the absence of light weighed heavily on her spirit. The tragic events of the extended weekend had taken their toll. What had been expected to be a few days of R&R and catching up with a friend, turned out to be nothing of the sort. The mental scars would last long after the physical injuries had healed.

With only the electronic glare from her gauges, Elizabeth longed to see the sun on the horizon; a sliver of natural light would do. She'd had enough of the darkness and everyone lurking in it. Judging from the clock on her dash, daylight would arrive just north of Portland. Right around Pennington Point.

Should she? Sunrises over the water were always spectacular there. As a child, she didn't appreciate the beauty of the views from the precipice. It wasn't until she'd been away at school for a period of time and returned home on break that she truly understood why people flocked to the Maine shore on annual pilgrimages. Before, it was simply where she'd grown up. Nothing special. And also the place she'd lost her parents. Perhaps that was why she'd gone so far away to attend college. And now she found it impossible to return.

Images of boarded-up windows and a front porch reduced to splinters hit her between the eyes. It had been nearly a year. She hadn't taken the time to drive up and check on the property that had been in her family for generations. *What condition would it be in? Could she ignore the pull and keep driving past?* She'd make the decision when she reached the exit.

The enduring heartache of losing her grandmother during the storm bubbled to the surface, so she poked at the radio dial to drown out the thoughts in her head. Morning radio with perky, chattering DJs. Not what she needed at the moment. Finally landing on a classical station out of Portland, she focused on reading the green overhead signs. If she did decide to turn off, she didn't want to miss the exit and have to double back.

Settling in for the long ride, Buddy stirred on the seat next to her, shifting his body up against the armrest and stretching his legs out with his paws pressed against the console. Elizabeth stroked his side, leaving her hand resting on it.

Sooner than expected, the first sign loomed ahead. PENNINGTON POINT 2 MILES. Decision time would come in two minutes. She busied herself with the radio again. Before long the second sign appeared. PENNINGTON POINT 1 MILE. *Should she pull off?* The sky behind her grew lighter. PENNINGTON POINT ½ MILE. She didn't want to go alone. She'd wait until she had someone to drag along with her. *But who would that be? Who was she kidding?* There was no one in her life that would be willing to drive five hours from Connecticut to go look at a property that was falling down and in shambles. But she couldn't do it alone. It would have to wait a little longer. It had waited this long. PENNINGTON POINT THIS EXIT. She let the green sign with an arrow pointing up and to the right go sailing by.

With an almost audible click inside her head, she slammed on the brakes, swerving into the breakdown lane. Buddy lurched forward, sliding off the seat with a yelp, landing on the floor with legs and paws flailing.

"Sorry, Bud." Elizabeth reached down and pulled on his collar, but he dug in his heels and resisted her attempts to get him back onto the seat. "How thoughtless of me. I'm sorry, Buddy." She stroked his head, but he cowered at her touch, shrinking back against the glove compartment. "Nice, Lizzi," she reprimanded herself. The last time she'd seen that look in her pup's eyes was the first time she saw him in his cage at the humane society. It gouged deep into her heart.

Knocking the stick shift into neutral, she kept her foot on the brake. The weight of her responsibility as the only surviving member of the Pennington family filled the small car like the surge of seawater pushed in from the tide. It was as if her grandmother had slipped in and taken the seat the pup had just slid off of. Struggling to keep her breathing steady, she tried to justify postponing her visit until another time.

"Damn it, Elizabeth. Don't miss this opportunity. You've got to do it sooner or later and you're right here. Right now." Jamming the shift into reverse, she was grateful the road was sparsely traveled at the early hour. Buddy tentatively climbed back onto the seat. "Sorry, big guy. I'll try to give you more warning next time." She stroked his head and he didn't withdraw this time. Backing the car up to the V where the exit lane veered off, she shifted back into first and sped down the ramp, merging onto a relatively quiet Route 1. Pulling into the right lane, she eased off the gas a bit.

Not too far down was Elizabeth's turn on Route 72, a winding, hilly road that wound its way through seven miles or so of pine trees, punctuated by the occasional dirt or gravel road that led to a residential dwelling tucked deep in the woods. A knitting shop, Dolly's Woolery, sat on one corner of Routes 1 and 72 and had been in the same location as long as she could remember. On the opposite corner was Ronnie's Clam Shack, popular with summer tourists as well as locals. She slowed the car and gazed longingly at the ice cream store next door. The hand-scrawled "SORRY WE'RE CLOSED FOR GOOD" sign propped up against the window from the inside stood in stark contrast with brightly colored cardboard pictures of ice cream cones, sundaes, and shakes. Her spirit sunk a bit deeper when she realized she'd never get a chance to have her favorite raspberry sorbet with dark chocolate chips again.

Kicking up dust behind her on 72, she followed the road as it snaked, taking in the simple beauty of the pines. Having spent so much time in the city, she'd nearly forgotten how majestic they were, standing tall and proud, feathery and deep green. After the last familiar curve, Elizabeth turned off 72 onto Pennington Road.

Cracking the window, she paused again to take in the salty sea air. It never got old. It was as if the Point was trying to coax her closer. She pressed on, down the familiar access road to the inn as it wound its way through an expanse of pines. Here and there, small trees had fallen along the sides, threatening to block the way, but she maneuvered around them. It didn't look like anyone had ventured down it since the last major storm. Then again, no one would have had a reason to. Once past the last fallen timber, the road opened up to a clearing on the precipice. In front of her was the open sea. To the left was the main building of the inn that faced out to the water. The condition of what she could see on the back of the building was encouraging; the damage appeared to be limited to a dangling gutter section and broken windows that were boarded up. In their haste to clear out before the hurricane hit, with no handyman available, windows had been left uncovered, leaving the inn vulnerable to nature's fury. Only after the storm were they covered to prevent further damage inside the buildings.

Elizabeth followed the circular drive around, rolling over healthy weeds that had been able to proliferate with no vehicles or pedestrians setting foot on the property for quite some time. As she pulled to the side facing the sea, all hopes for a swift renovation were dashed. The front clearly had taken the brunt of the storm. It was worse than she'd remembered from the day she drove away after her grandmother's funeral—boards on the windows merely masking the jagged edges of glass remaining in the frames. The roof of the porch had been stripped off and the railings left in splinters. The lawn was so overgrown, the bottom three steps to the porch weren't visible.

Grabbing a small flashlight from her glove box, she stepped out of her car, surveying the property in a 360-degree swath. It pained her to see it in its current condition. It was barely recognizable, like it had been years instead of months since the hurricane. Her pup pushed his way out the door with her, tail wagging and nose to the ground. He was not about to be left behind for this stop. This was new territory to explore.

Out on the end of the breakwater, the lighthouse still stood stalwart as it had for years against storms encroaching from the sea. It had also been her form of refuge as a child, heading out across the jagged rocks to find solace within the one-hundred-year-old walls, a peaceful place to hide and try to figure out life as an orphan.

The eastern sky had grown lighter since she'd exited the highway. The bright orange orb would soon make its way above the horizon. Sliding onto the warm hood of her car, she called her pup over, wary of him exploring too far without her. Spectacular rays suddenly splayed out across the water, making her squint and wish she'd thought to grab her sunglasses. The sunrise was lost on Buddy who wandered off, following a scent.

Once the sun had fully established itself in the firmament, Elizabeth slid off her car and headed for the inn, calling her pup away from something terribly interesting in the bushes along the cliff. She cringed at the thought of the drop-off on the other side.

Slogging through the tall weeds, she made her way toward the porch. *Would the steps support her weight? What would she find inside?* At the foot of the stairs, she hesitated. *Did she really want to see?* It could only be a stark reminder of what had been taken from her. Her childhood home. Her sweet grandmother. Her parents. Her innocence.

But now she was there. She'd taken the exit. She had to take a look. Tiptoeing up the rickety steps, she was horrified to see the far end of the porch had fallen in.

A key, deep from within her purse, brushed clean of the accumulated lint, slid its way into the slot. She hadn't thought she would use it so soon, but she found herself on destiny's doorstep. When it turned with a click, she pulled back, half expecting it to stop short of its duty. Her body jolted. The memories flooded back.

Oh, why was she here? Did she really want to see the storm damage wreaked on her beloved childhood home?

If nothing else, she needed to take a look as the sole heir to the property. Her grandmother would want her to, *wouldn't she? Would she be disappointed she'd stayed away for so long? Could she possibly understand the professional responsibilities she'd been struggling with? The hours she'd had to work? Hell, who was she to complain?* Her grandmother, Amelia, worked tirelessly day in and day out, to maintain the upmost quality of the inn's accommodations. It was hard to follow in her footsteps. Perhaps that was what she was afraid of.

When the knob turned without challenge, Elizabeth was almost disappointed it was so easy to get in. When she had needed a safe place to hunker down during the storm, it was like a fortress blocking her entry. She pushed open the door and took a tentative step, crunching in sand. Mustiness accosted her nose and crawled inside, threatening to linger. In the center of the small foyer, the turned-wood table that used to display opulent floral arrangements from Amelia's garden rested on its side with a shattered vase scattered in a v-shaped pattern on the floor like someone had pushed it over. Remnants of bygone floral stems had begun to decompose among the ceramic shards.

A flick of the light switches just inside produced nothing but a click-click, click-click. What had been a sparkling cut glass chandelier hanging from the center of the ceiling, remained dark with several prisms missing. The power had been turned off until an electrician could be brought in to check the wiring and perform any necessary repairs. To the right of the foyer, the only light in an otherwise dim space spilled into the sitting room from a window frame missing its plywood cover. Had someone pried it off? Gained access to the inn? Or had it simply fallen off in a subsequent storm with fierce winds?

Some of the furniture had been pushed to the far side along the fireplace wall to accommodate porch chairs and Schwinn bikes jammed in to keep them from becoming projectiles during the storm. A ladies' version near the large doorway lay on its side as if thrown down by a child who had lost interest and scampered off to another distraction. The upholstered pieces had taken on the briny smell of the ocean. She pulled off a piece of dried seaweed dangling from the arm of a chair and tossed it aside. It was clear the entire room had been drenched in seawater blown in through the broken windows, along with sand, plant life, and broken shells. Nothing could be salvaged. She'd have to start over if she were going to open the inn again one day. That decision still needed to be made, but her motivation for taking on the monumental task was deteriorating with each step she took.

There was an eeriness to the quiet within the inn. She'd never felt it so still. And she half expected her grandmother to pop behind the reception desk and greet her with the same exuberance she'd had her entire life. Her positive energy was contagious. Elizabeth longed to see her again, have her back, feel her arms around her. She missed her dearly. She didn't remember her own mother—or father—but she'd grown close to her grandmother who had raised her. Now her loss had carved a gaping hole in Elizabeth's heart, one she'd spent the last several months trying to ignore. It suddenly became more than she could contain. Grabbing onto the back of a faded floral wingback, her knees buckled and she dropped into a heap on the floor, sobbing. God, she missed the normalcy the inn had offered. A quiet place for guests to recharge, a home for her and her family.

A firm hand on her shoulder snapped her out of her downward spiral of gloom. As she spun on her heels, the unseen fingers slipped away. She pulled back, looking for the source of the sensation. No one was in sight, and she hadn't brushed against anything.

"Who is it?" she whispered. Her mind ran down the list of who'd passed away on the property. It could be one of several people. *Lord please let it be Amelia . . . or at least someone friendly.*

She pulled herself up onto wobbly feet, brushing sand from her palms. The interior was disturbingly awry. Her grandmother would be devastated if she could see it. Mold speckled the walls in an odd pattern that crept from the front door to the registration desk.

Did she dare venture any farther? Her pup nosed against her leg as if to question what they were doing there.

"I know, Bud. It wasn't what I was expecting either. This is awful. I had no idea it was this bad inside. It will take so much work—and money—to restore it to its former glory. I can't imagine taking on a project like this by myself."

She thought about how lonely it would be, too. With the nearest neighbors nearly two miles away from the property that stretched 125 acres, it would be desolate there alone on the precipice. She shrugged off a chill. Even if she decided she could hire out the work and oversee it from a distance, she didn't exactly have a lot of extra money lying around. She was in the throes of building her design business in Connecticut, a venture she'd longed to embark on and was finally fulfilling the dream.

Curious about the condition of the kitchen, a high-dollar-value area that could be the deal breaker if it was a total gut job, she headed through the dining room, switching on the flashlight with a click that echoed. She navigated through overturned tables and chairs, shuffling through sand scattered on the creaky wide-planked floor. Her pup hesitated to follow, whimpering as he lay down in the doorway.

"I'll just be a minute, Bud. Hang out there. I'll be right back."

The swinging door was harder to push than she remembered, and the familiar squeak was gone, as if the life had been stripped from it. Running her light from one end of the kitchen to the other, she was pleased it looked like they were simply experiencing a power outage. Nothing looked out of place with the exception of the big pots that usually hung from large hooks above the over-sized commercial stove in the middle of the space. Someone had stacked them neatly upside-down on the counter on the far side under a row of windows. There was a strange odor permeating the room that Elizabeth couldn't place. Briny seawater combined with cooking grease? Her voice of reason cautioned her that more serious complications could lie beneath what was visible.

As she rounded the end of the work surface connected to the stove, circling back through the kitchen, her eyes went to the wine cooler. Next to it was the entrance to the makeshift wine cellar that had been fashioned from a section of the tunnels beneath the inn. Years earlier when the property functioned as an all-girls school, a labyrinth of passageways was constructed to allow students to traverse between buildings without having to go outside, a veritable necessity during the harsh winter months on the coast of Maine. After the school's closing and the property was converted to an inn, most of the tunnels were closed off with the exception of the area directly below the kitchen. The constant cool temperature within the rock walls made it an ideal location for the inn's wine cellar. Elizabeth shuddered at her memories of exploring those tunnels.

Something sticking out from under the door to the cellar caught her eye. Inching closer, she could make out the dried-up tail of some sort of fish, conjuring disturbing images of its journey there and its slow, painful demise.

Curious how the wine inventory, another high-value area, had fared in the storm, Elizabeth yanked on the old tarnished brass knob. The door moaned as it let go of the frame, releasing a musty odor that was stronger than usual. Shining her flashlight into the murkiness below, the primitive wooden stairs appeared intact. Dark bottles lying on their sides lined the rudimentary shelves, rendering a sense of familiarity Elizabeth craved.

Venturing down for a closer look, she let out a shriek when a third of the way down, the steps gave way, sending her plummeting, landing in a heap on the cold, damp floor. The frame of the stairs tumbled with her, knocking her on the head before rolling off to the side. The flashlight slipped from her hand, throwing the cellar back into darkness when it hit the floor.

"*Damn it.*"

Scrambling to find her light, she got to her hands and knees, running her fingers in a widening circle around her, groping gingerly around the splintered pieces of stairway.

"Oh, come on. Where is it?" A whimper came from the top of the stairs. "Bud, stay. I'll be fine. Stay," she called firmly, hoping he wouldn't do anything rash trying to help her.

At last, her fingertips struck a hard cylindrical object. Snatching up the light, she flicked it back on, grateful it still worked after the fall. Elizabeth recalled how terrifying it was the time she got caught in the tunnels with a faulty flashlight and had no desire to repeat the ordeal. Shining the light up to her pup, she repeated her command to stay. In the beam, she could see the stairway had ripped clean from the threshold, allowing her no chance of climbing back up. She ran the light along the displaced and broken frame. There wasn't a section left that was large enough to lean against the wall to enable her to climb out.

"Good god. I've done it again." This time, there was no one else around for miles. "Bud, you're going to have to wait there. I've got to find a way out."

She reached to her back pocket for her phone, horrified to discover she'd left it in her car.

"And I guess I'm on my own to make it happen."

CHAPTER TWENTY-EIGHT

esperate to find a way back out through the doorway she'd fallen from, Elizabeth shined the light around her. She needed something to brace against the wall to climb up on. It didn't have to reach all the way to the top, just far enough for her to grab onto something and pull herself up.

The wine racks were all that occupied the immediate space. If she removed the bottles in one of the sections, could she drag it over and make that work? Moving closer she examined the back of the nearest one. It had been bolted to the wall to keep it from tipping over on the uneven ground.

Remembering the staff used to use a section of the tunnel to store extra chairs, she rounded a corner and stopped short. Not a chair in sight. Apparently they'd been brought up for Amelia's funeral yet never returned. She thought of tossing up a rope or some sort of strong cord to drape on the doorknob to pull herself up, but there was nothing she could find that resembled a line.

With no foreseeable way to get out the way she came, she resigned herself to making her way through the dark, dank tunnel to let herself out through one of the far-flung access points. Or had they been secured from the outside when the inn was boarded up after the hurricane? She'd find out when she got there. God, she hated the idea of venturing into the tunnels alone, but with no other obvious options, she had to try. No one knew she was there.

Giving a final command instructing her pup to stay put, she headed down the shaft toward what was left of Acadia House. The anxious canine let out a concerned yelp, and she assured him she'd be okay. She only wished she believed her own words. She prayed he wouldn't try to jump down into the tunnel, counting on his somewhat cowardly side to restrain him.

Acadia was one of two outlying buildings originally used as dormitories. The other structure burned down but was never rebuilt. The tunnel led out from the inn and forked partway out; one tine ended up at Acadia, which was later converted to guest suites, and the other eventually arrived at an abrupt dead end. Once the inn was up and running and the demand for rooms justified building a new wing, Moosehead Lodge was built near the footprint of the destroyed dorm but never connected to the tunnels.

Constructed of New England fieldstones, the tunnel measured approximately eight feet high by ten feet wide at the largest sections, but there were smaller areas constricted by underground rock ledges. Construction had been long and arduous yet critical to the success of the school. Rudimentary lighting installed to facilitate the students' passage through the tunnels had long since ceased operating. A well-functioning flashlight or lantern was now a prerequisite for venturing into the depths.

Crisscrossing her beam from wall to wall, ceiling to floor, she endeavored not to let the narrow width of the passageway and low ceiling height get into her head. She ran her palm along one wall in an effort to keep it from closing in on her. The rough stones were cold and damp. She shook off a shiver and kept going.

Not far down the shaft, she slowed her steps as her light caught a small mound of something dark. It looked furry—like some sort of small animal that had met its demise, perhaps unable to escape the tunnels once it had found its way there. Elizabeth prayed she wouldn't suffer the same fate. *Why had she felt the need to descend those damn stairs?*

Around the next bend, she came upon a pile of rubble the size of her car with part of a support beam sticking out of it, the splintered end pointing upward toward a hollowed-out section of earth. "So that's what happened," she whispered. Her fingers found the scar on the back of her head. Anxious to reach the end of the tunnel, she climbed over the pile, casting a wary look to the damaged ceiling, and picked up her pace.

As she neared the hatchway, a cough echoed in the tunnel behind her. Who was down in the depths with her? Dashing the last few yards, Elizabeth shined her light on the cement steps leading out of the tunnel. Lunging for what she prayed was her way out, she slid the sluggish latch and pushed on the doors but couldn't make them budge. Frantic, she made several more attempts, each one more forceful than before, throwing her body against them. Clearly they were secured from the outside.

Light danced on the walls behind her. She spun around with her back to the stairway, trapped with no way to defend herself. The light flashed into her eyes. She shined hers in the direction it came from onto a pudgy face. It belonged to the local police chief, and he had his gun drawn.

"Elizabeth?"

"Chief Austin, it's you. How did you know I was down here?"

"I didn't. You got lucky." He jammed his revolver back into its holster. "I check on the place from time to time, and I noticed the car, but you threw me off with the Connecticut plates. Thought I better take a look. Found the pup waiting anxiously at the doorway and the stairway in splinters, so I grabbed a ladder from the utility shed."

"Thank God you came when you did."

Once they were safely out of the tunnels, into the familiar space of the kitchen, Elizabeth hugged her pup whose back end wiggled with excitement and doubtless relief. She also grabbed the chief in an awkward hug, grateful he'd rescued her from certain death.

"I can't thank you enough. I was foolish to venture down into the tunnels. Don't know what compelled me to do it."

"Elizabeth, where have you been?" Leading the way back out through the dining room, he sounded like a father scolding his daughter for arriving home late, disappointed in her lack of judgment. "You haven't been back here since your grandmother's funeral, have you?"

A familiar nagging twinge resurfaced as she shook her head, ashamed to admit the truth and annoyed he'd pressed her. "I've been quite busy. I moved from the city and started my own—"

"Elizabeth, just *look* at this place." His palm chopped in the air toward the walls of the foyer. "Your grandmother would be horrified to see it in this condition."

Pulling away slightly, she raised a hand to signal for him to ease up, but he was far from finished.

"You can't do this. You can't turn your back on this place and leave it to fall into ruins. Not only is this your childhood home, it's an icon of this community. But now it's become an eyesore. Townsfolk are embarrassed . . . saddened by it. Not only that, it directly affects their livelihood. Guests of the inn used to go into town and shop and go out to dinner. Go out for ice cream with their kids. Take one of the boat trips to see the lighthouses or the seals."

The chief's words hit a disquieting chord. She hadn't considered the impact on the town. She hadn't been able to think past her pain.

His eyes went to her pup who was keeping a watchful eye on him.

"If you let it go too long, there will be no salvaging it. For God's sake, Elizabeth, you grew up here." His hands found their place on his hips as he straightened his back.

"All right already. I know. . . . Don't think I haven't thought of this place every day since I left. It's extremely painful. So much has been taken from me here. I couldn't stand the thought of returning. There's nothing left for me. It's become a sad reminder of all the bad memories."

"Well, the condition it's in doesn't help matters. If you fixed it up, the way it used to be, the way Amelia kept it, it would remind you of the happy memories. I know you have plenty of those. They may be tucked away right now, but you could unearth them as you return the inn to its former condition. . . . Fix it up. If you don't want to keep it after that—then fine. You owe it to your grandmother—the Pennington family—as well as this community. Sell it if you want, but no one will want it the way it is."

Horrified at his idea of selling the place, she couldn't think of a comeback to his rant. How could he be so flippant about getting rid of the inn? She couldn't possibly do that. Clearly he'd made his point.

The chief pushed open the front door, stepping gingerly onto the porch boards, looking as though he had put on even more excess weight since their last meeting. Elizabeth hoped she wouldn't have to help extricate him from falling through.

She knew he was right about the inn's condition but didn't want to hear it. It was easier to walk away and make excuses. His words cut deep yet rang true. Her nana would be appalled to see the inn in its current state and disappointed her Lizzi had let it fall into such squalid disrepair.

"And I can't keep coming out here to check on the place. It takes me away from more important matters." His voice trailed off as he headed toward his patrol car. Grabbing the door handle, he turned back. "Great to see you, Elizabeth. Hope you're not a stranger around here anymore."

Drawing in the salty sea air, she conceded, "I guess I won't be." Her pup's brown eyes looked up to her for direction as he nudged against her leg. "C'mon, Bud. I think I've seen enough." She tugged on his collar, and he trotted obediently next to her down the steps. By the time she ran back and locked up, he was sitting next to the passenger side door, waiting to be let in. She made a pass through the bushes along the front to see if she could locate the missing piece of plywood. It was nowhere to be found.

CHAPTER TWENTY-NINE

Partially hidden in the shadows of the doorway to her building, a man leaned against the brick wall, arms folded across his chest. Buddy stopped short, tilting his head, growling softly, his twitching nose high in the air. Elizabeth stepped off the curb but advanced no farther, holding her position next to her pup. Before long the man emerged, and she recognized the warm, friendly face. Placing her hand on Buddy's head, she assured him it was okay. He obediently sat down at her feet, keeping an eye on the stranger.

"Well, hello." A familiar tingling crept into her stomach. *Had he really walked back into her life after all this time?* Her eyes brimmed, and her throat grew tight, making it difficult to swallow.

He grinned and crossed the street toward her. "It's been a while." He slipped his arm around her waist and all pulmonary function shut down.

Wiping the corners of her eyes, Elizabeth cocked her head in amusement, thrilled to see him. "Kurt Mitchell." She drew in an uneven breath. "I can't believe you're here. It's so good to see you." She allowed him to pull her closer, lingering in their embrace, lost in time. Finally they pulled back far enough so their eyes connected again.

"Ya know, I used to think I was pretty good at my job. Following leads and tracking down someone of interest. But you certainly put me to the test." His smile went crooked, revealing a dimple. "I got this far, and then you disappeared."

"All the resources and technology available to an FBI agent and you failed to locate me until now?" She needed to push back a bit but lamented how far she went as soon as the words crossed her lips.

His torso stiffened. It was almost indiscernible, yet she could sense him pulling away from her. "I can't use those resources. That would be so damn illegal. Agents have gotten arrested for less."

She admired his integrity and aversion to jail time. "Of course. . . . I wasn't serious."

He loosened a bit. "But seriously, I called your office on Friday and just as you answered, I dropped my phone and it hung up the call."

"That was you?"

"Yeah."

"Well, that's been happening a lot, and it started to get to me."

"It might have something to do with your phone number. Did you know if you transpose the last two digits, you'd get Overeaters Anonymous?"

"Sounds like you're talking from experience."

"Yeah, I did it a couple times before I figured out what I was doing. Others could be doing the same thing."

"May be."

"And I tried your cell a number of times, but it doesn't seem to be working."

"No, I got rid of that number. I wanted to sever my ties when I left the city."

"Thank you for going out of your way to cover your trail."

"I honestly never expected you to come after me."

"Well, I did. . . . So how was your weekend?"

Elizabeth was relieved to see the glint in his eye had returned. She considered the sordid events of the long weekend she'd managed to survive. "Let's go grab a drink, and I'll fill you in."

"It's four in the afternoon."

"Okay, we can make it coffee. After the weekend I've had, though, I'm ready for a drink. In fact, I've got a chilled bottle of wine in my fridge." She reached down and took hold of a pinkie finger and guided him down the sidewalk, giving him a side glance, quite pleased he had tracked her down. Buddy trotted along behind them, tail wagging with contentment.

CHAPTER THIRTY

In the weeks that passed after her harrowing weekend in the deceptively tranquil harbor town, Elizabeth did her best to put the memories behind her. All her efforts were dashed when her phone rang one afternoon. Hoping it was a client, or better yet Kurt, she didn't recognize the number displayed in the readout. The area code, however, was quite familiar. Maine.

Gathering her most professional, yet lilting voice, she answered. "Elizabeth Pennington."

"*Elizabeth.*" The female voice was upbeat but didn't register right away. "It's Lucretia."

"Lucretia. Is everything all right?" She regretted her lead-in before she'd finished the question. Of course, everything wasn't all right. Fortunately, Lucretia didn't interpret it literally.

"Yeah, I just wanted to call and say hello."

"So good to hear from you. How are you doing?" It was as if she was talking to someone who had returned from the dead.

"Oh, I've been better, but at least the visible wounds are healing."

"That's good to hear. You're a strong woman in so many ways."

"Aw, that's very sweet of you. You are, as well."

Elizabeth appreciated the return endorsement but didn't feel she emulated the sentiment.

"Glad you're doing better." Images she'd tried to suppress crept back in. "Lucretia . . . I'm so sorry about Ana." Silence hung at the other end.

After clearing her throat, Lucretia stammered on her first word. "Yeah, that's been pretty tough. I miss her so much."

"I'm so sorry," Elizabeth repeated, mortified she couldn't come up with anything else to comfort her.

"That tears at me the most. Of all the wretched things he did, that cut the deepest. He knew it would."

Elizabeth allowed a pause to pay proper homage to her loss. Her friend had suffered unimaginable pain, both physical and psychological, at the hands of an evil man she thought she loved— and shared a bed with.

Yearning to move to a more pleasant topic and intrigued to learn the reason for Lucretia's call, she redirected her. "So how are things at The Inn on Boothbay Harbor?"

"As you can imagine, we've been going through a period of flux. I haven't been able to take over full-time at the helm yet, so I saw it as a good time to close down again for a bit and take care of those renovations we talked about. Ya know, get the décor back to my taste. I'm also going to rename it. There's been too much confusion with The Inn at Boothbay, so I've decided to call it Livingston Inn."

"That's great to hear. I just hope you're not taking on too much, especially since you're still recovering." Elizabeth paused, hoping the purpose of Lucretia's call wasn't to ask for her help. She had her Connecticut clients to keep happy.

"Oh, I've got help. Don't worry."

"You do?"

"Yes, I've decided to bring my brother into the business."

"Your brother?" Elizabeth didn't remember anyone mentioning a brother. She thought Lucretia was an only child.

"Yeah. Ben."

"Ben's your brother?" She hadn't seen that coming.

"He's my *half*-brother. Turns out my father had a son out of wedlock before he met my mother. I don't think he ever knew he had a son. Ben's mother headed out to Montana to give birth and raise him there, where she had family. I can't imagine how difficult it must have been to raise a child as a single mom. Once he found out about his father, apparently all he could think about was finding him. After his mother passed away, there was nothing to keep him in Montana, so he headed east."

Elizabeth thought of the letter she found from Lucretia's adoptive mother but couldn't bring herself to tell her Ben wasn't related to her. Not by blood, anyway. At the moment, though, he was the only connection to family she had. Elizabeth knew too well what it was like to live with the pervasive desolation from losing all those dear to her. She wouldn't wish that on anyone. Still, Ben's motives weren't clear. "Was he hoping to get written into the will?" Elizabeth didn't care if her friend considered her question crass. She wanted to be sure Lucretia was thinking the situation through. Was he really who he said he was?

"I think initially it was all about money and his share, but it quickly became more about establishing a relationship with his father. That's why he took on a job before revealing who he was to them. He undoubtedly had no idea how he would be received by either my mother or father. Unfortunately, they passed away before he could tell them."

"Why couldn't he be upfront with them?"

"He was going to tell them. He needed more time. He wanted to prove himself first without the stigma of being an illegitimate son who had just walked into their lives. I think he really wanted my father—our father—to love him as a son."

"So after your parents passed, how did he get the job as a bartender? Weren't some people suspicious of him?"

"Well, as I said before, people will talk. And it's not productive talk. . . . He knew the owner of the bar."

"How did that come about?"

"Oh, Elizabeth. The questions."

"I'm sorry if I'm digging deeper than you'd like to go. I'm concerned for you. You've been through several traumatic events recently, which you're still recovering from. I'm hoping you're making good decisions for yourself and not getting talked into anything that's not in your best interests."

"Ben wouldn't let me do that."

Elizabeth hesitated after her friend's declaration, hoping she could hear how ridiculous it sounded. It didn't have the effect she was hoping for. She kept going.

"Lucretia, hear me out on this. I know Ben is family—your half-brother—but how well do you really know him?"

"I know him very well."

Elizabeth ignored her defensive tone. "So how does he know the owner of Chauncey's?"

There was a soft exhale on the other end of the line. "This is not common knowledge in town, so please keep it to yourself."

"Okay."

"The owner's daughter was in a drug rehab program. He met Ben when he was picking her up at one of the group therapy meetings."

Elizabeth straightened up in her chair. "Ben was in rehab?"

"Yes—oh, but it's not what you're thinking. He wasn't a patient. He volunteers his time. It's his way of helping others after seeing what his mother went through—without any help. He also gives out his phone number to patients so if they're ever having a weak moment, they can call him. Sometimes he drops everything and runs to help them."

"That's pretty cool. . . . Wait, the owner's daughter." The only female she'd seen around Chauncey's was—"Ana?"

There was a muffled throat click and then a breathless, "Yes."

"Oh, Lucretia, I had no idea. I'm sorry."

"Yeah, it was so hard seeing her go through that. She had a tough time coming back home after graduation. The town was too small for her. She'd dreamed of traveling and ending up in some exotic place. When it didn't turn out that way, she turned to drugs to escape. But she'd been doing well lately, which was so good to see."

Elizabeth could only nod along in silence like a street reporter waiting for her cue to start talking on the six o'clock news. No words came to her.

"I honestly don't know why she came all the way back here. Her parents were thrilled. I was ecstatic."

She didn't have the heart to tell Lucretia she was the reason Ana came back.

"I don't think she and Ben got along all that well. Maybe she was afraid he would spill her secret. What she didn't know was her father had asked Ben to keep an eye on her, which he took to heart."

"He did? On a bicycle?"

Lucretia giggled at the notion. "No, silly. He and Edward were good friends, and he let Ben borrow his truck when he needed it. I lent Ben my camera to document Ana's whereabouts for her father because I knew she was behaving."

"That was very generous of him."

"It was. Ed was a very sweet guy. I really miss him, too. He didn't deserve what he got, that's for sure."

"I'm sure he didn't. . . . Did they ever find his body?"

"Yeah, Jonathon had buried him in the dirt floor of the carriage house, so Mack was able to figure out where, and they—"

"Oh, that's awful."

"Yeah, and I'm not so sure he would have been found if Mack hadn't been there to put a halt to pouring a new concrete floor."

"So at what point did you and Ben meet?"

"It was fairly recently. I was kinda shocked when he reached out to me."

"I'll bet."

"'Course we had to meet in private. I didn't dare run the risk of Jonathon seeing us together and getting the wrong idea. Not with his jealous temper."

"How did you know Ben was being truthful and not just someone looking to get something from you?"

"I have to admit I did question his motives. Although he did show me a certified birth certificate . . . and he does have my father's eyes."

"Why did it take him so long to approach you?"

"He said it took him a while to process the reality that our father died before he'd had the chance to connect with him. He considered heading back to Montana but then decided he should at least get to know me."

Elizabeth flashed back to images of the cemetery and the desecrated graves.

"I figured he'd be in jail by now."

Lucretia let out another girlish giggle. "In jail? What did he do to you?"

"Nothing to me. But I was with him when the chief caught him in the cemetery behind the inn."

"That was all a terrible misunderstanding. It was Jonathon who was digging up the graves and stealing from them. Apparently pilfering the family silver wasn't enough. Ben had discovered the mess and was trying to clean it up."

"Jonathon did that?" Was there nothing that sinister man wouldn't commit?

"Yeah, we found stuff he'd taken from the property and stashed up in the carriage house loft. And that section of the cellar that had been sealed off, that I understand you found, contained stuff he'd bought by running it through the inn's books. He had control of the checkbook. Wouldn't let anyone near it. No wonder we were struggling to make a go of it. . . . Won't let that happen again. They even found a bag of antique buttons in one of the cottages that was still under renovation. Apparently he stayed out of sight there after he murdered Edward. They think he picked up those buttons from his last trip, and they inspired him to start digging in our cemetery."

"Really."

"Yeah, he was a sick man."

"For sure."

"Ben's going to help me restore the cemetery to its original state and maintain the area going forward. It's finally going to be a space that my ancestors would be proud of."

"That's awesome. What about the stuff extracted from the graves? What's going to happen to it?" The deplorable lengths Sterling had gone to, to retrieve the antique trinkets, sickened her.

"We're going to donate them and the bag Jonathon brought back from Europe to the historical society in town and the antiquities museum in Portland."

"That's great to hear. I'm sure they'd love the donation." As her thoughts turned to her last encounter with Sterling, she fingered the back of her head where he'd clocked her with some sort of blunt object and dragged her into the back of a van. The wound had healed nicely, but she'd never forget the clod who had given it to her. "So I imagine Jonathon is withering in jail right about now. Has a court date been set?"

"Jonathon? You mean his brother, Robert."

"No. Jonathon. It may have been dark and I didn't see his face, but I didn't have to. I know what I heard. It was Jonathon's voice."

"Yeah, they sound a lot alike. But it was Robert who grabbed you. Guess he had plans to take care of who he thought was the only person who knew he was in town and connected to Jonathon. He thought he'd already eliminated me. But Jonathon . . . he's gone."

Elizabeth snatched a short breath. "So they never found him." It was as much a statement as a question.

"No. And at this point, I don't think they ever will."

"Wait a minute. Then how could Jonathon have murdered Ana? The timing doesn't seem to work out. I bumped into Ana the afternoon after he disappeared. Sunday afternoon. In the carriage house."

"Are you sure?"

Elizabeth thought back to her extended weekend in Boothbay Harbor. She could have sworn she was correct in her recollection, but perhaps she wasn't. The details had become fuzzy since she'd returned to more familiar surroundings, undoubtedly in an act of self-preservation.

"I could be wrong. I'm sorry. I don't really remember all the events so clearly anymore. Sorry to have questioned that." If she was right, it could mean Jonathon was still lurking about—or at least he had been until he completed everything on his perverse agenda.

Elizabeth prayed Lucretia was right.

"Lucretia, my heart goes out to you with everything you've been through. I wish you the best as you rebuild your life. You've endured more than most could ever imagine."

"I appreciate our friendship, and I hope you will visit again soon. I would love to get to know you better. And Elizabeth . . . you can call me Lucy."

ABOUT THE AUTHOR

National award winning author Penny Goetjen writes murder mysteries where the milieu play as prominent a role as the engaging characters. A self-proclaimed eccentric known for writing late into the night, transfixed by the allure of flickering candlelight, Ms. Goetjen embraces the writing process, unaware what will confront her at the next turn. She rides the journey with her characters, often as surprised as her readers to see how the story unfolds. Fascinated with the paranormal, she usually weaves a subtle, unexpected twist into her stories. When her husband is asked how he feels about his wife writing murder mysteries, he answers with a wink, "I sleep with one eye open."